LOVER

BETROTHED #3

PENELOPE SKY

Hartwick Publishing

Lover

Copyright © 2020 by Penelope Sky

CONTENTS

HADES

THE MEN LET ME PASS AS I STEPPED INTO DAMIEN'S HOME. His maid tried to talk to me, ask if I was staying for dinner, but I ignored her and sprinted up the stairs. I let myself into his bedroom and walked inside to the sight of him clean from a recent shower.

Damien stood in his sweatpants, his hair flat and wet. "What the hell are you—"

"Maddox has Sofia." Both of my lungs burst like balloons just from saying those words, admitting the truth out loud. My knees wanted to buckle underneath me and let me collapse to the floor. Instead of being livid someone had crossed me, which was my typical response, I was too broken to feel anything but unimaginable pain.

I couldn't think about what he was doing to her—because I might kill myself.

When Damien had processed what I said, his bad temper disappeared and his shoulders dropped with devastation.

"What?" His voice came out as a painful whisper, as if he were just as haunted by the revelation. "What are you talking about? Hasn't she been home this entire time?"

"I don't know how the fuck it happened, but it happened."

"Are you sure she's not—"

"No, asshole. He called me."

His eyes closed for a moment. "Shit."

My shaky legs couldn't hold me up any longer. I fell into the armchair next to the table. I couldn't even make myself a glass of scotch because I wouldn't be able to keep the drink steady. I was shaking with rage, trembling with agony.

Damien stepped closer to me, his face blank because he couldn't believe what he'd just heard.

I leaned forward with my elbows on my knees, my hands planted against my mouth.

Damien stood there for a while, ingesting the painful silence around us. After he went through the same emotions I had already experienced, he fell into the chair beside me. He sighed quietly, his fingers brushing through his damp hair. "We'll get her back, Hades."

"How?" My voice was so deep, I sounded demonic. "I have no idea where the fuck he is. I don't even know how long he's had her. If I knew where he was, I'd be there right now." I covered my face with my hands, feeling the tears burn behind my eyelids. I'd never cried as an adult, not even as a teenager, but now I was a pile of uncontrollable emotions. I knew I loved Sofia, but until that moment, I had no idea how deep my devotion ran.

"We'll figure it out."

"We've never been able to figure it out before," I spat.

"This time, we will."

"But it won't be quick enough to stop him before…" My voice cracked from the emotion, and I shut my eyes so I wouldn't have to picture what he would do to her, what he would do to my wife. I'd rather die by a knife to the gut than let that happen to her.

Damien was silent, just as disturbed as I was. He wouldn't dare mock me for my tears, for being a man with emotions.

I couldn't believe this was happening. I wanted to punch myself in the face in the hope I would wake up from this nightmare.

"There's no trade we could make?" he asked. "There has to be something he wants."

"No…" Because there was nothing better than her. She was the highest prize, the best way to hurt me, the best way to torture me. "My only hope is to steal her back…and kill that motherfucker."

"We'll figure it out, Hades. One way or another, we will."

I leaned back in the chair and sniffed loudly. The back of my hand absentmindedly wiped away my tears.

"I'm sorry…" Damien's voice broke with an audible choke.

All of this happened because of him—because he didn't fucking listen to me. "The only reason that I haven't killed you is because I need you. Everything that is happening to Sofia is your fault. Her blood and tears are on your hands." I turned my gaze toward him to look him in the eye. "I lost my wife because of you, and even if we get her back, I'll never forgive you."

2

SOFIA

I WAS ON THE SECOND STORY OF A LARGE HOUSE, SOMEWHERE in the middle of western Tuscany. Once I'd been transported to the location, I was thrown into a bedroom. The large windows were barred shut, and the bedroom door was impenetrable.

I sat on the bed, leaned up against the headboard, my knees pulled to my chest. My arms were crossed over my stomach, and I kept my eyes on the door. I wasn't in a grungy cell, but I knew I was a prisoner all the same. It was only a matter of time before Maddox came for me, either to kill me—or to do something worse.

I hadn't cried or showed any emotion yet. I was doing my best to stay strong, to convince myself that Hades would find a way to get me back. I recalled him saying he could never track down Maddox, that the man was impossible to trace.

So what if he never found me?

Or maybe it didn't matter; maybe Maddox planned to kill me at any moment.

I hoped Maddox wanted to make a trade. Maybe there was something he wanted from Hades, something they could exchange for my life. Whatever it was, Hades would do it. He would do whatever was necessary to get me home.

The wedding ring rested on my left hand, the only comfort I had while I sat in this foreign bedroom. It reminded me that I was part of something greater, that there was someone out there who would do anything to save me.

I knew it was nighttime because I could see the darkness through the windows. I had no idea what time it was because there wasn't a clock in the room. My phone had been confiscated sometime after I passed out. Maybe it'd been a whole day, or maybe it'd been only a few hours.

Heavy footsteps sounded outside the door, and it seemed like a man was headed my way. My body automatically tightened, giving in to the fear of what would happen next. I wasn't oblivious to Maddox's attraction to me. Maybe he only wanted me because I belonged to Hades, but that made me just as unsafe.

The door opened, and he entered. Wearing jeans and a gray t-shirt, he quietly shut the door. His gaze moved to me on the bed, and he stared at me with expressionless eyes. His hands slid into his pockets, and he stared at me for moments, hardly blinking.

He hadn't touched me, but that look made me feel violated.

I was rigid on the bed, my heart beating fast because I was ready for another fight. I could feel the pulse in my ears, feel a sense of danger in my fingertips. My eyes were as focused on his as his were on mine.

He eventually pushed off from the door and crept toward me, his hands slowly sliding out of his pockets. He moved to the edge of the bed and helped himself to a seat.

I automatically pulled my legs closer to my body, trying to stay as far away from him as possible.

His eyes were focused on me again, the blue color burning like frost. The most alien part about him was his lack of need to blink. He could stare endlessly for minutes straight. Sometimes, he didn't even seem human because of the trait. It was innately creepy.

I was terrified. I did my best to be brave and pretend I didn't feel anything, but deep down in my soul, I knew Hades couldn't protect me right now. He wasn't hiding in the shadows, ready to come to my rescue. I couldn't rely on his protection anymore—and that was when I realized how much I needed him.

And how alone I was.

Maddox turned his gaze to his hands. "I'm sorry it has to be this way."

"If you're sorry, just let me go."

"You know I can't do that. You know I'll never let you go. You know I'll do terrible things to you—because I know it'll hurt him the most. Your husband is my greatest adversary. We have a love-hate relationship. He encroaches on my turf, kills my brother, and doesn't keep his word...but I also respect him. He's a good opponent. I suspect he'll be an even better opponent now that this is happening."

This guy was a psychopath. "I'm sure Hades will give you whatever you want if you let me go."

"But this is what I want—you."

I started to shake.

"I want to hurt him, to punish him. There's no better way to do that."

This couldn't be happening.

"But I realize you're an innocent person. You just made a mistake when you married him."

There was a glimmer of hope in my heart that this man had some compassion.

He reached into the back of his jeans and pulled out a pistol.

Shit.

"So, I'm going to give you a way out." He held up the gun. "It's got one bullet—and that's all you need."

My heart started to beat even harder. If my only way out was suicide, then I was in a worse spot than I realized. If death was preferable to his torture, then this gesture may be compassionate after all. "And if I say no?"

"I'll pity you. But I suspect you'll change your mind later… The offer is always on the table." He returned the gun to the back of his jeans, and his hands rested on his thighs. "Having the liberty to claim your own life is a gift. That's the only compassion you'll get from me."

I'd never been a crier, never been the type of person to let people watch me bleed, but this was so disturbing, I wanted to sob in heartbreak. I was scared…more scared than I'd ever been in my life. There was no way out of this unless I took his offer. "What will you do to me?"

He moved his eyes to my legs and slowly lifted his gaze up my body. The arousal in his look was unmistakable, his intention clear as day. He wanted to claim me as his own, turn me into a slave.

I was going to be sick. "Please don't do this…"

"I was a gentleman and gave you a way out."

"No, you're not a gentleman. Gentlemen don't…" I couldn't bring myself to say the word. "Hades will come for me. He'll slaughter you and everyone you know."

"I hope he does. But even if that day comes, it's gonna take him a long time to hunt me down. If he knew where I was, he would've killed me a long time ago."

I tried to control my breathing, but it was becoming more labored. My throat started to itch; my eyes began to water. I couldn't keep up my strong resilience, not when I felt so helpless and alone. Crying and begging wouldn't save me, but I felt the impulsive need to break down.

"I'm sorry about this," he whispered. "I really am."

The tears started. I pulled my body tighter, trying to be as small as possible.

He rose to his feet and pulled off his shirt. "Resist me, and I'll hurt you."

Now, I sobbed. Sobbed because there was nothing I could do. If Hades knew what was happening to me, he would kill himself just to make the pain stop. If my mother knew what was happening to me, she would never recover. I was tempted to take that gun just so I could keep my dignity. No one would judge me if I took the easy way out.

But if I did…I would never see Hades again.

And Hades would have to live with my blood on his hands.

I had to live…just in case he did find me.

When I closed my eyes, I decided not to open them again, not until this was over.

3

HADES

I SAT ON THE COUCH IN MY BEDROOM. I'D BEEN SITTING there for so long that the darkness had crept in the windows and brought my room into shadow. I hadn't gotten up to flick on the lights. I hadn't even gotten a drink.

Scotch wouldn't help.

My phone was gripped in my hand, waiting for information from my men. They were following every lead possible, torturing any man who might possibly know where Maddox could be. Every phone call I'd received led nowhere.

We had no idea where he was.

No idea where my wife was.

It'd been three days since she disappeared, three days that she'd been subjected to cruelty. I couldn't sleep, couldn't eat. I was so sick to my stomach I threw up a couple times. All I could think about was what he was doing to her.

That I didn't save her.

I wished we'd never met. I wished she married someone else. If she had, none of this would have happened.

I was supposed to keep her safe, but all this was happening because of me.

I closed my eyes and rubbed my temple, feeling physical pain everywhere. My muscles were sore from running around, my head pounded because I hadn't eaten, and my neck was tight from my face being constantly tilted toward the ground.

But my pain couldn't possibly compare to hers.

My bedroom door opened, and I didn't bother to look at who it was. It was probably Damien, there to deliver bad news.

A deep voice I recognized erupted across the room. "Helena told me to walk inside."

It took me a moment to raise my chin and look at him. I could recognize that voice anywhere, because I'd been listening to it since I was a child. When my eyes landed on his face, they narrowed. I knew who it was, but it took me a moment to believe what I was seeing.

Ash stepped farther into my bedroom, an apologetic look in his eyes.

"Why are you here?" Reestablishing a relationship with him was at the bottom of my priorities. Alive or dead, I couldn't care less. The one person in the world who actually mattered to me was missing. I couldn't sleep in my bed, not when I had no idea where she was sleeping, when I had no idea how she was being treated.

Ash took a seat beside me, leaving several inches of space between us. With his elbows on his knees, he stared straight ahead. "Damien called me."

I didn't see why. "You didn't need to come all the way down here."

"Thought I could help."

"Why would you want to help me?" I shouldn't be so spiteful, but I was too depressed to care about my behavior.

"You know why."

"I really don't. You made it clear that you hate me."

"I don't hate you. And I certainly don't hate your wife. We're a family…and I'm here for you."

It was ironic that my brother was sitting beside me, that he'd dropped his venom and put aside our differences. I couldn't get him to give me a chance whatsoever, and now he was there, being a brother, being a friend. "I'll take all the help I can get."

"Any idea where he could be?"

I sighed in annoyance. "If I did, I wouldn't be here. I wouldn't be sitting on my ass in the dark."

Ash wasn't a smartass in response. "Any leads? Any moles?"

"I've checked them all…nothing."

"We'll keep looking," Ash said. "I'm with you on this…til the end."

I dragged my hands down my face, furious that I had no idea how to fix this. My wife was the victim of god-knows-what, and I was sitting on my ass doing nothing. I pulled my hands away and let a few tears escape. I loved this woman so much that I would smile if I could take her place. Loving her was like living with my heart outside my body. It was vulnerable, delicate, and she carried it in her hand. Whatever happened to her happened to me.

Ash glanced at me from the corner of his eye before he wrapped his arm around my shoulders, giving me affection I hadn't expected. We hadn't embraced each other as brothers in over five years. As if my father hadn't been killed by my hand, he was loyal to me. He was there for me. "I'm sorry, man. You don't deserve this."

"I'm surprised you would say that."

"You shouldn't be." He gently rubbed my back before he dropped his hand. "It's time we leave the past in the past. Mom and Dad are gone, but we have each other. Let's move on—starting now."

I turned my gaze to meet his look, my eyes wide because I couldn't believe what he'd just said. "Does that mean…that you forgive me?" I spoke the question out loud, unable to believe we were having this conversation at all.

"Yeah," he said quietly. "I do."

Instead of feeling joy, I felt devastation. I'd accomplished what I set out to do, but it didn't make any difference at all. My wife wasn't here. She couldn't love me when she was being tortured and god-knew-what.

Or if she was dead.

His statement only made me feel worse, made me feel like I'd lost even more.

4

SOFIA

IT STARTED TO FEEL LIKE FALL.

The trees and meadow in the distance were changing colors. The deep green of summer slowly faded to autumn, tints of red and yellow. I sat on the balcony and tried to focus on the innate beauty around me. If I focused hard enough, I wouldn't have to think about my own reality.

What I had to do every night.

I stayed in this bedroom and took my meals on the balcony. I wasn't allowed to leave, so this room became my whole world. When I looked across the countryside, sometimes I imagined that I saw Hades and his men coming for me, in armored trucks and with weapons.

But then I blinked and realized it was a hallucination.

As every night passed and my mind became more disturbed, I considered the option Maddox had offered me.

All I had to do was pull the trigger.

If no one cared about me, I'd probably do it, but Hades would never recover. My mother would be alone. And Maddox would win. I had to stay alive long enough to be saved. I had to have faith that Hades would come.

I couldn't give up on him.

Not when he would never give up on me.

So I blocked everything out of my mind and pretended this wasn't happening. I became my own therapist, trained myself to repress the horror that was taking place. If I compartmentalized everything, I could pretend it wasn't happening at all.

Footsteps sounded behind me, and I recognized their heaviness. They usually only came during the night, but it was the middle of the day now.

Maddox fell into the chair beside me, his knees wide apart as he stretched out. He surveyed the countryside in front of him, as if he were more interested in the view than he was in me.

My heart started to palpitate. I hated being close to him, hated being in the same vicinity. I crossed my legs and immediately shifted my body away from him. I did my best to not think about the horrible things he was doing to me, but when he was right beside me, that was impossible to do.

He sat in silence for a long time, enjoying the quiet companionship.

I wanted him to leave, so I stayed quiet in the hope he would eventually walk off.

But he stayed.

I finally spoke. "Is there something I can help you with?" I didn't want this man to infringe on my peaceful afternoon, on the time designated for myself. The abrasive woman inside me wanted to throw him out of my bedroom, but this guy was freakishly strong. It was best not to provoke him.

"No."

I stared straight ahead and hoped he would leave on his own.

"Are you enjoying your time here?"

It was so ridiculous, I almost did a double take. "Is that a serious question?"

"You live in a nice house, have chef-prepared meals, and look at this view. It could be worse."

"No, it couldn't be worse."

Both of his arms rested on the chair, and he propped one ankle on the opposite knee. He was dressed casually, a long-sleeved shirt and jeans. "Maybe I need to step up my game."

I knew I should've kept my mouth shut. "How long are you gonna keep me here?"

He turned his gaze toward me. "Forever."

I felt the blood drain from my face; I felt my fingers squeeze an invisible trigger. "You got your revenge. No need to make this situation permanent."

"I'll decide that."

I wasn't sure how long I'd been there. Perhaps it'd been a week, maybe two. It was ironic that I'd lost track of time even though I had nothing else to do. I would give anything to hear my husband's voice again, to be connected to something good. He probably had no idea if I was alive or dead. "Can I talk to him?"

His face remained blank. "Why?"

"I want him to know I'm okay."

"But are you okay?"

"Well, I'm not dead…yet."

He faced forward again, dismissing my request.

I tried again. "Please." It was unlikely that I could tell Hades where I was, that Hades could figure out my location, but maybe it was worth a shot.

He looked at me again. "And why should I?"

"Like you said, I'm innocent."

He considered my request for several minutes before he reached into his pocket and grabbed his phone. He typed in a number and made the call.

I held my breath because this actually might work. I might get to talk to Hades again.

Maddox smiled just before he began to speak. "How are you, Hades?" He continued to smile as he listened to whatever Hades said in response.

I couldn't hear a single word.

"Your wife wishes to speak to you. Should I put her on?"

My hands turned slippery once my palms began to sweat. I ached to take that phone, to feel safe, even for a few seconds.

Maddox extended the phone to me, a warning in his eyes. "One minute. Say something stupid, and I'll kill you."

I took the phone with a shaky hand and brought it to my ear. My heart was racing in ecstasy, wrestling with the unbridled joy this moment could bring. I took a deep breath before I spoke my first word. "Hades?"

Hades was quiet on the line, as if he didn't hear what I said. Only his breathing was audible, noticeably strained, noticeably profound. When he spoke, his voice came out as a strained whisper. "Baby?" All he said was my nickname, and that was enough to show how devastated he was. His agony was audible, his pain visible like colors on a spectrum.

Now I wished I'd never called.

He didn't ask where I was, probably because he knew I couldn't answer. Even if I could answer him, I really had no idea where I was. Instead, he gave me hope to keep living. "I'm going to get you out of there. I promise."

My eyes watered as I gave a slight nod, not that he could see me.

"Just stay strong for me a little while longer."

I was too emotional to speak.

"Baby?"

I didn't tell him how miserable I was. I didn't tell him what Maddox was doing to me. It was best to say nothing at all. "I miss you…"

After a painful sigh, he said, "I miss you too."

I had been so excited to talk to him, but once I had him on the phone, I didn't know what to say.

"Baby…are you doing okay?" He didn't ask anything specific, probably because he didn't want to know. It was the vaguest question he could ask.

Tears streaked down my cheeks and I tasted them on my lips, but I kept the pain muffled so he would have no idea. "Yeah…I'm okay. I can't wait to see you. I can't wait to come home."

"You'll be home soon. I promise."

Maddox snatched the phone out of my hand and ended the call. "Did that make you feel better?"

No—it made me feel worse.

5

HADES

I SAT ON THE PATIO OUTSIDE MY BEDROOM WITH MY TWO greatest allies.

Damien and Ash.

That phone call had been brutal. She barely said a few words, because she didn't want me to know how much she was suffering. She was trying to make me feel better when I was the one who should be making her feel better. I'd managed to steady my tears, that way she wouldn't have to listen to me break down. I played that conversation over and over in my head, and every time I did, it sounded worse.

I had to get her out of there.

Damien leaned back in his chair, his cheek propped on his hand. "She didn't give you any hint to where she was?"

I shook my head. "No."

"You couldn't trace the call?" Ash asked.

"No. We only talked for a minute." I rubbed my finger against my temple, needing this agony to end as soon as possible. I did my best to get a location on her, having my men search everywhere, but we had no leads. I had friends all over the globe, but none of those friends could help me.

Because Maddox had no friends. No one had any idea where he was—since he never told anyone.

Even though Damien was also part of the business, Maddox had always been focused on me. He was obsessed with my nature, obsessed with my brutality. He had a sick fascination with my character. Damien never seemed to matter to him. It'd been that way for many years.

"I think I know what I'm going to do." I stared straight ahead and avoided the looks of the two men.

"You've got a plan?" Damien asked. "Let's hear it."

It wasn't really a plan...more of a surrender. "I'm the one he's obsessed with. I'm the one he wants to humiliate. I'm the one who fascinates him."

Ash cocked an eyebrow. "Where is this going?"

"I'm gonna make a trade—her for me." If he'd wanted me in the first place, he would've taken me. He didn't because he knew my wife was a better choice. But maybe now he might change his mind. Maybe I could talk him into letting me take her place.

Damien leaned forward. "If you do that, he'll kill you."

I nodded. "I'm aware."

Damien couldn't hide his unease at the idea. He couldn't picture his life without me. "But if you die, she's going to be miserable."

"She's miserable now, Damien." I'd rather die than let my wife be a prisoner to another man.

Ash stared at me but remained silent.

"I'm out of options," I said. "I'm not even sure he'll go for it. But if we keep searching at this pace, it'll be years before we find her. And I don't have years."

Damien still had disagreement on his face, but he didn't challenge me. "You should really think this through before you make that offer."

"I already have." I grabbed the phone and made the call. It only rang a few times before he answered.

"Hades, to what do I owe the pleasure?" He was enjoying this far too much, so much that he probably wouldn't trade her for anything.

"You and I have been at war for years. You invaded my territory, and I fought back. We could do this dance forever, and unfortunately, we probably will. But I think we should settle this once and for all. I want to surrender to you... completely." Just making that statement was humiliating. But I didn't have time for pride. I had to do whatever was necessary to get Sofia out of there. "Take my surrender,

Maddox. I'm the one you want. Let her go and take me instead."

"If I wanted you, I could've taken you a long time ago."

"But not like this. I'll get on my knees and bow to you. You can beat the shit out of me, and I won't fight back. You can do anything to me, and I won't resist. I'll be your puppet, and you'll be the master. You've broken my will, broken my soul, so you won. Take your prize." I stared at nothing in particular as I waited for a response, as I waited for him to say what I wanted to hear. I was handing over my death in exchange for Sofia's life, but for me, that was a small price to pay.

Both men stared at me, waiting for the outcome of the conversation.

Maddox took his time answering, slowly considering my offer. When he finally gave his answer, the smile in his voice was long gone. "Alright. You have a deal."

———

I sat in the back of the SUV, Damien up against the window. The cars drove down the road that wound through the countryside. It was two in the morning, pitch black outside. When the brigade found the dirt road in the field, we made a left and disappeared into the landscape. Once we changed terrain, the vehicles shifted left and right as the ride became bumpy.

I should be afraid of what was about to happen.

But I was only relieved.

Sofia would be free, and the second she was out of sight, I'd probably have a bullet between the eyes.

That was fine with me.

Damien would take care of my widow. She would inherit all of my assets. My last name would still protect her.

Or maybe the prophecy would protect me. We were supposed to have two sons. If I died tonight, that couldn't happen. I didn't picture myself believing in such bullshit, but now I held on to the fantasy like a religion.

There was still hope.

The string of cars drove farther into the countryside, the meeting point miles away from the closest building. Our lights would be invisible from the main road. Our gunshots would be absorbed by the trees.

After a few minutes, we arrived at the meeting spot. Maddox was already there with his team of mercenaries. All the vehicles were lined up, facing us with their headlights on. Just like last time, Maddox leaned against the hood of a car, his arms crossed over his chest. That wicked smile was on his face...like a fucking clown.

Our car stopped, and I stared at him through the windshield, feeling a furnace of white-hot rage burning me from the inside out. My nostrils flared like they were about to emit fire. My knuckles ached as my hands formed tight fists. I'd never wanted to kill someone so much in my life.

I knew what he'd done to Sofia… I didn't even have to ask.

I would never kill an innocent person, but I wished he had someone he loved just so I could do the same thing to him. There was no line I wouldn't cross, no crime I was afraid to commit.

I'd lost my mind.

I sat there for a moment longer, calming my urge to kill. I had to walk out there and surrender to this maniac. I had to get on my knees like a pussy so my wife could go free. I had to sacrifice my reputation, my credibility, everything for the woman I loved.

But I would do anything for her.

"Hades?" Damien's quiet voice came from the other side of the car. He spoke quietly, as if he were afraid someone might hear us.

I knew we were about to say goodbye to each other. Once I handed myself over to Maddox, I would never come back. I was angry with Damien for being the catalyst that caused all of this, but in a moment of weakness, I actually felt pain. I turned my gaze to him.

"Let me take your place."

I'd been expecting a handshake or an emotional goodbye. But not that.

"This is all my fault. It should be me."

I stared at the sincerity in his eyes and knew he was being serious.

"You and Sofia should be together. And I should pay for what I've done."

Even though he deserved that punishment, that was the last thing I wanted. I couldn't let my best friend take my place. "No."

"Hades, come on."

"I said no."

"I want to do this." His eyes started to fill with moisture, the most emotion he had ever shown. The lights from the cars reflected in his eyes, showing the way they swirled with agony. His breaths quickened, his chest rising and falling rapidly.

I looked away because I couldn't stand the sight. "She's my wife. It has to be me. This is what I signed up for when I married her. It's my job to sacrifice everything for her." I looked outside and saw no signs of her. She was probably hidden in the back seat somewhere. "I'd die for her a million times."

"You need to live so you can take care of her."

"She can take care of herself. The only reason she's ever been in danger is because of me."

"No…because of me."

"I know you'll look after her, Damien."

He gave a slight nod, taking a deep breath to steady his pain.

I turned back to him. "Just get her out of here, alright? I don't want her to see anything."

Damien struggled harder to control his impending tears. "You shouldn't be alone. No one deserves to die alone…"

"Knowing that she's safe is all I need." Now that there was nothing left to say, it was time to get out of the car and face my death like a man. I didn't want to say goodbye to Damien. How did you say goodbye to someone you loved? I extended my hand to shake his. "Good luck, asshole." I did my best to lighten the mood, to make this easier for both of us.

Damien didn't comply. He pushed my hand away then moved across the seat so he could embrace me. He hugged me tightly and patted me on the back. "I love you, asshole."

I closed my eyes for a second and swallowed the emotion that wanted to explode inside my throat. I gripped the back of his shirt tightly and let the air slowly leave my nostrils. "Yeah…I love you too."

We both exited the car and headed to the no-man's-land between us. Damien stayed a few feet back with my men.

Despite the agony in every single muscle of my body, I stood strong and proud. My shoulders were squared, and I held my head high, taking my execution like a man looking forward to greeting death. My eyes locked on to Maddox's, unafraid.

Maddox straightened and took a step closer to me. "Are you ready?"

Regardless of what I was about to face, I'd never been more ready in my life. "Let her go."

"You're lucky I actually keep my word." He nodded to one of his men.

A pair of guys went to a vehicle in the back and dragged her from the back seat. They each held her by one arm as they escorted her forward. They dragged her until she stood beside Maddox, and once her eyes were on me, a look of relief stretched over her face. I'd come to save her, come to take her home. Her hair was messy because she didn't style it anymore, and her face was free of makeup. But she didn't have a single bruise or mark...and that made me so grateful.

I wanted to stare at her forever, but I had a job to do. I looked at Maddox again. "Let's do this."

Maddox grabbed her by the arm and gave her a light push forward. "Go, sweetheart."

As if she couldn't control herself, she ran straight into my arms. The momentum made me stagger back for just a second. Somehow, she still smelled the same, like roses and lilies. Her face moved into my shoulder, and she took a deep breath as her arms circled my waist. A few tears escaped, soaking my t-shirt.

My arms circled her body automatically, and I squeezed her tightly, so thankful I got to have this one last moment with her. It made everything worth it, made my punishment easier to accept. And it made me realize how much I truly loved her. I'd been a selfish man all my life, but once I had her, there was no me. Only her.

I leaned back slightly so I could press a kiss to her forehead. My hands slid into the back of her hair, and I cradled her against me, letting my lips soak up her taste. I didn't want to let her go, not ever, but I had to let her go…forever.

Maddox grew impatient. "Now, your end of the deal."

I grabbed her arm lightly and tugged her aside. "Get in the car, baby."

She glanced at Maddox before she looked at me. "You aren't coming?"

I didn't have the courage to tell her what was about to happen.

She was so damn smart that she figured it out on her own. Her eyes flooded with tears, and she started to panic. "No." She grabbed me by the arm. "No, don't do this." She began to sob, delirious. "I'll stay with Maddox…" Tears streaked down her cheeks, making rivers on her skin. The moisture in her eyes was more noticeable because it reflected the headlights like bright beacons.

When she went on an emotional rampage, I couldn't look at her anymore. "Damien."

She turned hysterical. "No. Please, no."

Damien stepped forward and took her by both arms.

She fought against him like she was fighting for her life, screaming at the top of her lungs. "No, don't do this!"

Damien hooked his arms around her waist and dragged her to the car.

When I couldn't see her anymore, I could hear her muffled screaming coming from inside the car. She pounded her fists against the window, trying to break free. She'd rather be a prisoner to Maddox than see me suffer.

I turned my gaze back to Maddox. "Wait until she leaves."

He stepped closer to me, that disgusting smile on his face. "This has been a lot more enjoyable than I thought it would be."

I listened to the engine start. Then I heard the cars turn around and drive away. Even over the sounds of the vehicles, I could hear her muffled screams. She probably begged Damien to turn around and come back for me.

I tried not to think about it anymore. Now I needed to stay strong and accept the outcome of my decision.

When they were long gone and we were alone, I took solace in the fact that Sofia was safe, that she wouldn't have to watch what was about to happen. She had another chance at life, a chance to start over.

Now, all I had to do was die.

Maddox motioned to one of his men. A second later, a wooden bat was placed in his hand.

So, he was going to beat me to death.

I would only think about Sofia until my body gave out.

Maddox tested the bat in his grip. "Anything you wanna say before we get started?"

I kept my mouth shut.

"I'm not going to kill you. I'm going to make you wish I would kill you."

6

SOFIA

"You need to calm down." Damien gripped me by both shoulders and forced me into the armchair in my bedroom. "It's done. No going back."

I slapped his hands away. "Don't tell me to calm down." Tears poured down my face and soaked my cheeks. "How could you let him do this? I'd rather live with Maddox for the rest of my life than let Hades sacrifice himself for me."

"Well, he wouldn't." He kneeled in front of me, his head slightly bent. His hair was messy, as if he'd fingered it all night long. His eyes were full of moisture, as if he were holding back tears. "I know this is hard. It's hard for me too, but this is what he wanted."

Watching Damien break down only made me feel worse. We'd both lost someone we loved. My chest heaved as I sobbed my heart out. "I'd rather be raped by Maddox a million times than let Hades die for me."

Damien pulled out a full syringe from his pocket. "I think you should take this."

I was in so much agony that I was tempted. I wanted to forget what had just happened; I wanted to forget watching Hades stand there as we drove away. Instead of being happy that I was home, I couldn't appreciate it at all.

Because Hades wasn't home.

"How could you let him do this?" I wiped my tears away with my fingertips. "How could you let him die for me?"

Damien bowed his head for a moment. "It was his decision. He couldn't live with himself, knowing what was happening to you. I tried to take his place, but he wouldn't let me."

"So, we do nothing?" I asked. "We just let him…"

"It's what he wanted."

"But what kind of life could I have without him?" Fresh tears fell down my cheeks.

"You can live a happy life, because that's what he wanted."

I eyed the syringe, but I decided not to take it. Hades had had to suffer constantly while I was away. He didn't take drugs to erase his pain. Neither would I. "Did Maddox say he would kill him?"

"Didn't specify."

"Then why did you drive away? Why did you leave him alone?"

"Because that was what he wanted."

"Do you think there's a chance he could be alive?" I knew how unlikely that was, but I couldn't stop myself from hoping, from believing. I wanted to believe there was a chance we would make it back to each other.

His response was a whisper. "I don't know."

"Could you drive back in the morning...just to check?"

Damien wouldn't dare deny me. "Of course."

When there was nothing left to say, we sat there in silence, both thinking about the man who meant so much to us. He was probably being tortured as we spoke, and that made me sick to my stomach.

"Ash is here."

"He is?" I asked.

Damien nodded. "Do you want to see him?"

Under normal circumstances, of course, but right now, I didn't want to see anybody. I was traumatized by what had happened, heartbroken by what I'd lost. It would be impossible to carry on a coherent conversation. "No."

"Alright." He rose to his feet and dug his hand into his pocket. When he pulled his palm out, he opened his fingers and revealed the black wedding ring Hades had worn every day since we got married. "He wanted me to give this to you..."

I gripped it in my shaky fingers and started to sob harder.

Hades knew he wasn't coming back.

I closed my fingers around it and squeezed. "Give me the syringe."

7

HADES

I KNEW IT WAS MORNING BECAUSE SUNLIGHT FILTERED through my eyelids.

I lay on the grass, my back against the dirt. My clothes were soaked with blood, and I could barely think because my mind was so fuzzy. So many things were broken, so much blood had been lost. I writhed in unspeakable pain, subjected to such agony that I knew Maddox was right.

I did wish I were dead.

I couldn't stand and walk; I couldn't even reach for my phone in my pocket. I was paralyzed on the ground. Even if I could grab my phone, I wasn't sure I could figure out how to call someone. My body was broken, and I couldn't move.

I would die here.

I had a few hours left, maybe more.

To distract myself from the pain, I thought of Sofia.

She was safe. She was home. She was free.

I could die happy.

The sound of approaching tires was recognizable to my ears. I was so delirious, I was probably hallucinating the whole thing. Maybe it was a fantasy, that someone was coming to rescue me. The likelihood someone had driven out into the middle of nowhere was nonexistent.

I stayed still on the ground with my eyes closed. I couldn't move anyway.

A car door shut, and boots thudded against the ground. It was a cold morning in the fall. My lungs ached with every breath I took.

"Fuck." The footsteps sounded hurried as someone ran over to me. "Hades?" One hand immediately went to my neck to check my pulse, while the other rested against my chest to check my breathing.

I forced my eyes to open, even though it was painful to do so. From between the slit in my eyelids, I could make out Damien's face.

"Holy shit." Damien looked over my body, examining my countless injuries. "I can't believe you're alive."

"I won't be much longer."

"Can you stand?"

I groaned in response.

"I'm going to get you to a hospital, okay? Just hold on." He pulled out his phone and made some calls. "Stay with me, okay?"

I was already slipping away.

Damien gave me a shake. "I need you to stay awake."

"I can't…"

"Don't do it for you. Do it for Sofia."

8

SOFIA

I DIDN'T GET OUT OF BED.

The sheets smelled just like him. If I kept my eyes closed, it was like he was still there. I stuck to his side of the bed and pretended he was there with me. His wedding ring sat on the nightstand, and I stared at it as the hours trickled by.

I didn't know what to do with myself. I'd never needed a man in my whole life, and now I didn't know what to do without this man.

I didn't know how to go on.

He wasn't just my husband, but my partner, my friend.

Everything.

Now he was gone.

A knock sounded on the door. "Sofia?" It was Damien's voice. He was probably there to check on me.

There was nothing he could do for me.

"I'm coming in." He opened the door and stepped inside the bedroom. He came over to the bed and didn't care that I was just in one of Hades's t-shirts. My privacy didn't seem important anymore. "Sofia, are you listening to me?"

My eyes were open, but I ignored him.

"I went back to the field, and I found him."

My eyes shifted to his. "What?" I pushed off the sheets and sat upright. He could see my underwear, but I didn't care. "Is he...?"

"He's alive...barely."

I stiffened. "Where is he?"

"I took him to the hospital right away. The doctors said he needs a lot of surgery. They took him to the OR immediately."

My hand covered my face like I was stifling my scream. My heart raced violently. Every part of my body hurt from excitement and anxiety. "So, he's going to be okay?"

"I don't know. No one knows right now."

I got out of bed and reached for my jeans on the floor. "We've got to head over there now."

"Sofia."

I stilled at the seriousness of his tone. "What?"

A large frown was on his face. "He told me he doesn't want you to see him right now."

My jeans fell to the floor. "What? I'm his wife."

"He just doesn't want you to see him like that. He's in really bad shape."

"I don't give a shit how he looks, he's my husband. I'm gonna be there for him."

Damien stepped closer to me and didn't dare look at my legs. "I'm just the messenger, okay? This is what he wants, and I'll let you know when he's ready to see you."

I knew Maddox must have hurt him badly, and Hades didn't want me to witness the horrible brutality. He didn't want me to witness the cruelty he experienced. He was just trying to protect me. The moment I looked at him, I knew I would feel guilty. He'd paid for my life with his own evisceration. "So, what am I supposed to do? Just sit here and wait?"

"I'll give you updates as soon as I get them."

I ran my fingers through my hair. Then I yanked it from my scalp. "He's my husband. I should be taking care of him."

"You will when he's ready." Both of his hands moved to my shoulders. "I know this is hard, but let's just be happy he is alive."

Tears welled in my eyes as I absorbed that blessing. Regardless of how he'd changed, Hades was still here. If he'd survived whatever Maddox put him through, he would survive this. He was the strongest man I knew. And I knew he was too proud to let himself appear weak in front of me, especially in a hospital bed.

"There's nothing you can do for him anyway. Nothing anyone can do. He needs to survive these surgeries and rest. He's a strong guy, so I'm sure he'll heal." Damien's hands dropped from my shoulders, and he brought me in for a hug. "We just have to be patient."

I sat on the balcony with my dinner in front of me. Helena had made me my favorite supper, but I wasn't hungry.

I was never hungry.

My phone sat beside me, and I constantly waited for it to ring. Damien gave me updates regularly, and so far, Hades had been unconscious most of the time. He'd had his left arm broken in several places, his ribs were cracked, and his right leg was fractured. Not to mention his other internal injuries.

Helena stepped onto the patio. "You need to eat sometime."

"I'm sorry. I'm just not hungry."

"Well, Mr. Lombardi would like you to eat."

She was right about that.

"Would company make you feel better?"

The only person I wanted to talk to was my husband.

"Ash is standing outside. Is it okay if I let him in?"

I forgot Ash was in the area. Damien had told me he'd come down to help, but I'd forgotten that information the second I heard it. "Sure."

Ash walked in a moment later, wearing a dark green shirt with a black jacket on top. He approached the table and looked down at me with a sad expression. His hand reached to my shoulder, and he gave me a gentle squeeze. "You doin' okay?"

"No."

"At least he's alive."

"He won't let me see him."

"No surprise there," Ash said. "He's always been that way. Doesn't want anyone to see him weak."

"He's not weak," I snapped, "He's hurt."

"He won't let me see him either, if that makes you feel better."

"No…"

Ash looked down at my untouched food. "Are you gonna eat that?"

I shook my head.

He pulled the plate toward him and grabbed a fork. "Looks good."

"Helena is an amazing cook."

"Then why aren't you eating?"

I shrugged. "Not hungry."

"How do you expect to take care of him if you don't take care of yourself first?" He took a bite and handed the fork back to me, as if we were going to share the meal.

I knew it was a ploy to get me to eat, but I caved anyway. "I'm surprised you came down here."

"When Damien told me what happened, I felt like shit." He leaned back into the chair and stared at me with sad eyes. "You didn't deserve to be taken, and despite my issues with my brother, he didn't deserve that horror. No man should have to lose his wife like that."

I knew Hades must have been miserable while I was gone. I didn't tell him what Maddox did to me, but I had a feeling he knew.

"One way or another, Maddox is gonna die. Either I'll kill him, Damien will, or Hades will. Fucker's gotta die."

"I should be the one to kill him." I would get a gun, load it with one bullet, and lock him in a cell so he had no other choice. He could either starve to death or end it quickly.

Ash gave a slight nod. "Yes, you deserve it. One day, we'll make it happen."

"They say tragedy brings people together. At least some good came out of this." Ash and Hades were talking once again, behaving like brothers. "He really wanted to make things right with you, and he was devastated when he couldn't."

"Did he ever tell you why it was so important to him?"

I didn't want to lie about his hunch that there was more to it; he was dead on about his assumption. "No. But it doesn't matter because his desire for reconciliation was genuine."

He turned his gaze away and stared over the balcony. "I guess it doesn't matter anymore. Life is too short for grudges."

"I couldn't agree more."

He turned his eyes back to me. "Is there anything I can do for you?"

"No. You can head home, and I'll give you updates when I receive them."

He shook his head. "I'm not going anywhere. When we finish this, I'll leave."

"Don't you have a business to run?" Not that I considered it to be much of a business.

He was quiet for a long time as he considered my question. He grabbed the fork off the plate and took another bite. "I thought about what my brother said... Maybe it's time to move on."

"What does that mean?"

"I'm not naïve. I know our father was an asshole. When I heard that Maddox had taken you, I was devastated. I'd only met you a couple of times, and I already cared about you. Knowing what Maddox was doing to you…made me sick to my stomach. It made me realize that I was no different from him, that I was a huge asshole. I don't want to be that guy anymore."

"Who do you want to be?" I whispered.

"Not sure yet."

"Will you work with Hades?"

"No. I want to do my own thing. I think I might be a pimp."

I laughed because I assumed it was a joke.

"I'm serious. It's basically what I was doing before, but now I'd work with girls who want to work. And I could protect them as a boss."

It was still an unconventional career choice, but at least he wouldn't be hurting anybody.

"I love women, sex, titties. You could say it's my passion in life." He shrugged slightly. "I'd rather do that than deal drugs."

It wasn't the most respectable line of work, but I could get on board with it. "That'll make Hades happy."

"He'd be really happy if he were still single. He'd want to use my services all the time."

I wasn't oblivious to Hades's behavior before we were married; it never bothered me. But now I was a bit jealous thinking about everyone who came before me. His sex life used to be a lot more adventurous. Now, he was tied down, committed to one woman. I wondered if he ever got bored. "Where are you staying?"

"In a hotel."

"You wanna stay here?" I asked. "We have a lot of extra bedrooms."

"Yeah, I can tell. This place is a mansion. A little big for just two people."

"Three."

His eyes glanced down at my stomach, an eyebrow raised.

"My mother lives with us," I explained.

The accusation disappeared from his eyes. "Do you want me to stay with you?"

After being violated by Maddox, I never felt safe anymore, especially with my husband gone. Knowing he was still out there made it impossible to sleep at night. Until he was dead and buried in the ground, I would never drop my guard. "If you don't mind…"

His eyes showed his sympathy. "No, I don't mind at all."

9

HADES

WHEN I OPENED MY EYES, I SAW THE WHITE CEILING ABOVE my head. Everything in the room was the same color—plain, boring white. The monitor next to the bed beeped as it kept track of my heart and blood pressure. The tube had been taken out of my throat once the surgeries were done, and I could finally breathe on my own. I was on a morphine drip, so I actually felt pretty good.

I wasn't sure how much time had passed, maybe a couple weeks. I'd been unconscious most of the time, so I really had no idea. Damien told me how hurt Sofia was when I refused to see her, but she didn't understand that I was doing her a favor.

It would kill her to see me like this.

"How are you doin', man?" Damien's voice came from beside me.

I turned my head toward him. "I'm on morphine, so pretty damn well."

He pulled the chair closer to the bedside and rested his arms on the rail. "I talked to the doctors. They relieved the pressure in your skull so the swelling could go down. They repaired your punctured spleen, and they fixed the fracture in your leg. You've got a couple bone bruises, but those will heal."

"I hate to imagine what I look like right now."

"Yeah…you look like shit."

I smiled slightly, because the drugs took the edge off. "Fuck you, asshole."

Damien rested his hand on my arm and gave me a slight pat. "I can tell you're doing better."

"That's the morphine talking."

"You've been on it for a couple weeks now, and you were never in this good of a mood."

I couldn't even remember the last few weeks. "How long have I been in here?"

"Over two weeks."

"How's Sofia?"

"Eager to see you."

I faced forward so I wouldn't have to meet his look.

"Ash is staying with her."

"He is?" I asked, slightly surprised. "I'm out of the picture, and he tries to steal my woman?"

He chuckled. "I don't think anyone could steal her from you."

"It was nice of him to keep an eye on her."

"Yeah. He seems pretty fond of Sofia. And he must be fond of you too."

"I'm surprised he's taken so much time off of work."

He shrugged. "You're more important, I guess."

"The doctors say when I can get out of here?"

"In another week or so."

What kind of shape would I be in when I walked out of here? Would I be able to walk? Would I be able to take care of myself? I hadn't actually seen myself in the mirror, so I had no idea what I looked like.

"I know it's not my place, but I think you should let Sofia come down here."

"You just said I look like shit."

"I know, but she's your wife. You need her, and honestly, she needs you too."

After everything she'd been through, she was probably disturbed, broken. I was the only person who could be there for her. I didn't want to hear the details of her suffering, but it was my job to put her back together. "I'm not sure if I can handle it…"

Damien bowed his head. "I can't even imagine."

Maybe that was the real reason I didn't want to see her. My physical injuries would heal, but her emotional scars would haunt us both for life. Every time I thought about it, I was riddled with guilt. I should've done something sooner; I should've protected my wife. I didn't have the balls to look her in the eye, not when I felt so worthless.

"But you should be together."

I missed her, I missed holding her hand, I missed looking at her beautiful face.

"Can I go ahead and call her?"

"I don't want her to see me like this."

"I'm sure she feels the same way." He pulled out his phone from his pocket. "But you're husband and wife… You belong together."

I sat up in bed and waited for her to walk inside. My heart was pounding like a drum, and my stomach was tight with unease. I was nervous—nervous I would look at her and burst into tears.

What if she didn't want me anymore?

What if we couldn't get past this?

What if she blamed me for what happened to her?

I was so afraid of losing her that I didn't know what to do.

She stepped inside my hospital room wearing a purple top and dark black jeans. She stilled when she spotted me in the bed, her eyes immediately filling with tears. It took her a second to process my condition, to overcome the shock of my appearance, but when she did, she came to my side.

She set her purse down then pulled her chair closer to the bedside.

When I looked at her face, I saw the same woman that I loved, the same beautiful and fiery woman I wanted to keep for the rest of my life. I didn't see Maddox in her gaze; I didn't see the things he'd done. My feelings for her were exactly the same.

The longer she stared at me, the more her eyes began to fill. "Oh my god…" Her hands reached for one of mine, and she squeezed it with both of hers. She took a deep breath to control her tears, but a few escaped anyway.

"I'm okay, baby."

She sniffled and more tears fell.

"We're going to be okay."

"You shouldn't have done this for me…"

I brought her hand to my lips and kissed her knuckles. "I would do it again in a heartbeat."

"We're gonna kill him," she whispered. "We're gonna burn him alive."

I loved seeing the fire in her eyes, that ferocity that made me fall in love with her in the first place. She had the same spirit, the same strength I found so endearing. "I know we will." I didn't feel the resentment in her gaze; I didn't feel the accusation or the blame. She looked at me just the way she used to...like nothing had changed at all.

She drew back her hand and opened her purse. She pulled out the black wedding ring I hadn't taken off since the day I became her husband. She grabbed my left hand and slid it back where it belonged. "Don't take this off again, okay?"

I squeezed her hand as the tears welled in my eyes. "Never."

SOFIA

I STAYED AT HIS BEDSIDE DAY AND NIGHT.

Most of the time, he wasn't awake. The drugs made him drift off to sleep, which was a good thing because he needed to rest. I sat by his side, putting new flowers in the room and helping him eat his meals. I didn't look at him differently in his weakened state.

And he didn't look at me differently either.

After a week had come and gone, the doctors said he could leave soon.

"You must be excited to go home." When I sat at his bedside, I always held his hand. Our fingers were locked together like a couple madly in love.

"I'm just excited to get out of bed."

"Well, don't expect to start running around again. You're going to be in bed at home too."

He rolled his eyes playfully. "Okay, nurse."

"I'm not a nurse. I'm your wife."

He squeezed my hand gently. "That's a lot sexier anyway."

I continued to hold his hand and stare at his face. His once perfect features were marred by bruises and discoloration. He'd had a skull fracture that needed to be repaired, so they'd had to shave his head. His hair had never been long, but he looked different with the shorter strands. Staying in bed caused him to get smaller because he wasn't working out anymore, so his body was slowly changing.

But he was my husband all the same.

Ash stepped inside the hospital room. "Smells like a funeral in here." He approached the bedside wearing a long-sleeved t-shirt and black jeans. With his hands in his pockets, he approached the bed and looked down at his brother. "I'm looking for Hades Lombardi... I must be in the wrong room."

Hades gave him a cold look. "Shut the hell up, asshole."

"Oh wait, that is you!" he said with a slight laugh. "You sound like a whiny bitch, just like my little brother."

This time, Hades couldn't slow the smile that slid across his lips.

Ash's smile faded away as he looked at his brother seriously. "You look like you're in good shape."

"It could be worse," Hades said. "But thanks for visiting on my last day here. That was convenient."

"You have a wife for that," Ash said. "I know you didn't want to see my ugly face."

"You're right," Hades said. "You do have an ugly face."

Ash turned to me next. "How are you doing, sweetheart?"

"I'm just happy he's okay." I brought his hand to my lips and rested it there.

Ash stared at me for a moment before he turned back to his brother. "So, you're going to be home tomorrow?"

"That's the plan," Hades answered.

"Does that mean I should move out? It's nice getting free meals from Helena and pleasant conversations with your mother-in-law." Ash stared down at his brother, slight playfulness in his eyes.

"No, you should stick around." Hades squeezed my hand. "Thanks for taking care of my wife while I've been out of commission."

"Oh, I've been taking care of her." Ash winked.

"I can get out of this bed and kick your ass," Hades threatened.

"Maybe if I let you," Ash said with a laugh.

Now that Ash had dropped their feud, I realized how lighthearted they could be. They were like any other brothers who teased each other all the time. It was nice to make a few jokes when things were so somber.

Ash turned serious. "Is there anything I can get you? Anything I can do?"

"No, man," Hades said. "You've done enough."

"Alright. Well, I'll see you tomorrow." Ash reached down and shook his brother's hand. "Only a real badass could've survived something like that. Hades, you're definitely a badass."

After being discharged by the doctor, Hades was free to go.

We gathered his medications, and instead of taking a wheelchair, he insisted on walking out on his own two feet. He disregarded the pain because he was so damn stubborn. He'd rather prove that nothing had changed even though he'd survived a traumatic experience.

Instead of nagging at him, I let him do whatever he wanted.

We returned to the house, and the stairs really slowed him down. He gripped the rail as he ascended to the second floor. Taking his time, he moved like a snail, and when he reached the top, he looked winded.

I wanted to help him, but he was too large for me to assist. "Stay here for a second."

He was clearly in pain because all he did was give a slight nod.

I went up to the third floor and knocked on Ash's door.

He opened it, wearing jeans and a t-shirt like he was about to go out. "Is the asshole home yet?"

"He's on the second floor… He's having a hard time."

Ash narrowed his eyes slightly, understanding my unspoken words immediately. He shut the door behind him and headed down the stairs to the second floor.

Hades stood there, still tall and proud. No injury would make him weak. Maybe he was stubborn…or maybe he just had too much pride.

When Ash reached the bottom of the stairs, he didn't make a smartass comment or put down his brother in any way. He grabbed his arm and threw it over his shoulder. "Let me give you a lift."

When Hades didn't reject the offer, it was clear he really needed help.

Together, the men made it to the third floor, and Ash escorted his brother into our bedroom.

When Hades was inside, he kicked off his shoes and took a seat in the armchair. He breathed slightly heavily, swallowing the exertion. He rubbed his hands together and bowed his head, as if to hide his visage.

I turned to Ash. "Thanks for the help."

"I'm always here." He didn't make any jokes like he normally would have. He turned away to give his brother privacy.

I shut the door and turned back to Hades. I watched him continue to sit there, his head bent toward the floor. He rubbed one knuckle absentmindedly, as if he was thinking about something else. The bedroom was clean, with fresh sheets and new flowers, something to make him feel at home. "Must be nice to be back, huh?"

He nodded slightly before he rose to his feet. He moved much slower than before, as if all of his muscles resisted the command. Once he was standing straight, he inhaled a deep breath. He struggled to pull off his shirt. When it was over his head, he tossed it aside. Thick gauze was wrapped around his torso to protect his ribs, and he still had swelling and discoloration all over his skin. He looked so much better now than he had before, but he still looked beaten.

I came to him and helped him with his jeans. I got his boxers off too, assuming he would want to take a shower now that he was home from the hospital.

I was surprised he allowed me to help.

Wordlessly, he slowly made his way into the bathroom and turned on the shower. He left the door cracked behind him.

I listened to the water fall for a few moments, wondering if he wanted to be alone. But I knew he'd been alone for weeks now, suffering in silence because he refused to let his guard down. Even if he wanted to be strong for me, he

shouldn't have to be. I was his wife. I should be at his side...
wherever he went.

I shed my clothes and then joined him in the shower. I came
up from behind and noticed the way he stood idly under the
warm water. With his eyes closed and droplets of water
dripping down the bridge of his nose and his hard chest, his
mind seemed to be far away.

When I shut the shower door, he tensed at the audible click.

I moved toward him and gently rested my forehead
between his shoulder blades. My arms circled around his
hips so I could avoid his sensitive ribs. He blocked all the
water, so I was cold, but I was happy just to be there. Happy
we were both there.

Hades stood still for a long time and didn't reciprocate my
affection. We'd had a tender moment together in the
hospital, but now, he was cold, like he wanted to be alone.
He was probably just in a lot of pain, but sometimes I feared
he felt differently toward me altogether.

Hades slowly turned around then pulled me under the
water with him. His brown eyes weren't as territorial as
they used to be, but deep affection still burned in his gaze.
His hands tightened on my lower back, and he pulled me
closer to him. Once my forehead was against his chest, he
rested his chin on top of my head.

Together, we stood under the water...silent.

We'd both suffered immense tragedies, the kind of agony
neither one of us could comprehend, but we comforted

each other the only way we knew how. We were still a team; we were still partners.

We were in this together.

For the first week, Hades didn't get much sleep.

When his pain meds wore off, he lay there in the dark, staring at the ceiling.

Somehow, I always knew when he was awake. The sound of his breathing was different, and it registered in my subconscious brain. During those moments, I would turn toward him and stay awake just so he wouldn't feel alone.

We hadn't talked about what happened yet…and it seemed like we never would.

During the day, he stayed in bed. Sometimes, he worked on his laptop or talked on the phone. He would have his morning coffee, but he wouldn't eat much as he was concerned about gaining weight with his newly sedentary lifestyle—even though it should be his last priority right now.

I stayed home with him, working on my laptop whenever he did and doing my best to be good company without smothering him. At night, we watched movies, switching back and forth between the chick flicks I liked and the mafia movies he liked.

He improved slowly—really slowly.

I was sitting at the table reading an email on my laptop when Hades spoke to me.

"You should go back to work." He sat up in bed, his back resting against a pile of pillows. He was shirtless, his flawless musculature still powerful under the scars. He'd stopped shaving, but the shadow looked good on his handsome face. He was moody every day, managing his pain in silence. He didn't talk much…not that he had before.

"Why would I do that?"

"Because you've been absent from work a long time. I'm sure you're eager to get back."

I had to stop myself from tilting my head because his statement was ridiculous. "I don't want to go anywhere, Hades. I want to stay here—with you."

He continued to hold my gaze with a stoic expression, but there was a hint of emotion in his eyes. He flicked his eyes away and stared out the patio doors. "There's nothing you can do for me. I have Helena."

"But I'm your wife. It's my job to take care of you—and I want to."

He kept his gaze out the glass doors. It was unclear if he was touched by that statement or not. He probably felt uncomfortable accepting my support, when he shouldn't.

"Besides…I don't want to put myself out there anyway." I never went into detail about my captivity, not just to protect him, but because I didn't want to relive the experience by discussing it. I'd rather just pretend it never happened.

His eyes returned to mine, his expression still hard. "He won't bother you…if that's what you're afraid of."

I'd always be afraid of it. "What makes you so sure?"

"Because I paid for your freedom. The transaction is complete." His eyes fell, like he was reliving the moment when he took my place.

If he said that was true, then it probably was. But my place was still next to him. "I'm going to be by your side until you get through this."

"I appreciate that, but I'm fine. Really." Considering the significant trauma he'd experienced, it was a miracle he was in such good shape. Maybe because he was so strong before the incident, he was able to get by relatively unscathed. "There's nothing you can do for me. And please don't pity me."

"I don't." My eyes narrowed. "How can I pity the strongest man I know?"

He wouldn't look at me.

There was a knock on the bedroom door.

I opened it and came face-to-face with Damien. Instead of talking across the threshold, I stepped into the hallway and shut the door behind me. "He's getting there… It's gonna take some time."

With his chin tilted toward the floor and his hands in his front pockets, he looked like a guilty dog that had destroyed the house before his owner returned. "Can I see him? Maybe we could have dinner tonight?"

"I don't know..."

"Please." He begged with his eyes. "Could you just ask him?"

I knew Hades didn't want to see anybody right now, but I couldn't deny Damien's request. "Let me see." I walked back into the bedroom and sat on the edge of the bed.

Hades didn't meet my look. "No." He must have heard Damien's voice through the door and already made up his mind.

"You haven't seen anyone..."

"I said no."

I continued to stare at my husband, seeing the rage in his eyes. He could convey such raw emotion with very little expression. Years ago, I couldn't read him, but now I understood even the slightest movements. "What happened between you two?"

"All of this happened because of him." He grabbed his left hand and massaged the knuckles of his fist, as if he fantasized about punching Damien in the face. "Tell him to leave me the fuck alone and not come back."

"I understand you're upset, but he didn't mean for any of this to happen. He's your best friend..."

"I don't give a shit what he meant to happen. He's no friend of mine."

"Hades…"

"Tell him to leave, or I will."

I knew he would make good on his threat, so I returned to the hallway. I closed the door behind me and crossed my arms over my chest. "He needs his space right now…"

Damien's eyes fell with devastation. "I know that's not what he said."

"Give it time. I'll talk to him."

He ran his fingers through his hair nervously. "It won't change anything. I fucked up."

"He's just angry right now. You know how he gets. If you give him enough time and space, he'll come around."

Damien shook his head slightly. "Not this time…"

HADES

My recovery was taking a lifetime.

I understood I needed to be patient...but I'd never been patient.

I took what I wanted, and if I couldn't, I made it happen. But I was at the mercy of God's design. This would take time, and there was a serious possibility that I would never be the same. My shoulder may always ache, my ribs may hiss with every breath, and I would never be quite as strong as I once was.

But it was worth it. I got my wife back... That was all that mattered.

Ash came to my bedroom for a visit. After Sofia let him inside, he approached the edge of my bed. "Haven't seen you in a while. Thought we could catch up."

My brother had been my enemy, and now he was my only friend in the world. Damien had been cut from my life with a butcher's knife. I never wanted to see that son of a bitch ever again. He'd ruined my life. I nodded to one of the armchairs. "Take a seat."

Sofia glanced back and forth at us before she slipped on her heels. "I'll leave you two alone."

I watched her grow four inches taller in the shoes. "You don't need to leave, baby."

"I should have dinner with my mom anyway." She moved to the door. "I'll be back in an hour or so."

Ash grabbed a bottle of scotch and made himself a drink. "You want one?"

"I wish."

"Oh, that's right." He took a seat next to me. "You're on all those pain killers." He tilted his head back and took a drink.

"Among other things…"

He licked his lips then stared at me for a long time. My brother wasn't afraid of eye contact. In fact, he thrived on it. "How are you?"

"Fine."

"That's not what I'm asking about." He set his glass on my nightstand, then settled into the chair. "You'll get over this… in time. A couple broken bones won't defeat you."

He was asking about the one thing I didn't want to talk about. "I'm not okay. I'll never be okay."

My brother's eyes shone with sympathy. "She seems to be alright. She's a strong girl."

"She's the strongest woman I know. But even if it didn't hurt her at all, it'll always kill me." I looked away because I didn't want this conversation to continue. I was angry with everyone, from Damien to Maddox. But I was angriest with myself.

What kind of man was I?

My one job was to protect my wife. I promised her I would. I promised that no one could ever touch her. Turned out, that was just a bunch of bullshit. I was a worthless human being, and I deserved to die in that field.

Ash took another drink then wiped his bottom lip with his thumb. "I'm sorry, man. I really am."

"I know you are."

"What's your next move?"

"Get back on my feet. Kill Maddox. It's pretty simple."

Ash gave a slight nod. "May not be that simple. He'll expect it."

"Doesn't make a difference. I'll get him one way or another."

"You got me and Damien behind you."

I hated hearing that fucker's name. If I didn't want to kill Maddox so badly, I would exclude him from everything. But I needed all hands on deck. Once we were done, I wouldn't need Damien for anything anymore. Then he could rot in hell. "You've stayed here long enough. I know you have a life to get back to."

"Not really." He shrugged. "I thought about what you said…"

"You want to be a partner?" That was perfect now that Damien wasn't part of my life anymore. I needed someone I could trust, someone who wasn't a complete idiot.

"No."

I cocked an eyebrow.

"My business interests have changed. Witnessing this whole thing has given me a change of heart. You're right, I don't want to be that guy…"

I couldn't believe what I was hearing. "Then what are you gonna do?"

"Be a pimp."

I gave a slight smile, but I couldn't tell if he was joking or not. "A pimp?" I asked incredulously.

"Yeah, it's perfect. It's pretty much what I was doing already."

"So, you're gonna have a bunch of prostitutes work for you, and you're gonna hand them out to clients?"

"Exactly. But in this case, the women are volunteers, and they make that moolah."

"And what about all the girls you already have?"

Ash grabbed his glass again. "They're free to go."

"You do realize that they'll turn you in?"

He shrugged. "Then what? You think the cops are gonna touch me? They're my biggest clients."

Being a pimp wasn't the most respectable line of work, but it was a dramatic improvement over what he was doing before. "Well, I think it's great."

"And if you were single, you'd think it was *really* great."

I gave a slight chuckle even though it hurt my ribs a bit. "I can't believe you're gonna be a pimp. It just sounds so ridiculous. Are you gonna get one of those bright purple suits?"

He couldn't hide the grin that crept onto his lips. "Shut the fuck up, bitch. Now you'll never see my best inventory."

"I already have the best inventory."

He winked. "Touché."

"Does that mean you'll be leaving, then?"

"Depends. If you need me, I'll stay. Not a bad idea to have me outside your door every night."

"I don't need any help, Ash."

He took a drink then set down the glass. "See, that's the problem. If you needed help, you would never ask for it."

No, I never would.

"So, I'll ask your wife what she thinks."

"I don't need my woman making decisions for me."

"When she's taking care of you, I disagree."

Sofia had been at my side day and night. Instead of going back to work and resuming her life, she chose to spend all of her time with me. She'd been a captive for an entire month, but now she was cooped up in a room all over again. When she'd brought my ring to the hospital, it touched me so deeply. Seeing the way she attended to me like a wife who loved her husband was exactly what I wanted. But it was still hard to let her see me in my weakest state.

"How much longer do you think you'll need?"

"It's gonna be at least a month."

"Damien and I can always take care of it."

I wanted Maddox dead, but I wanted to be the one to kill him. "No. I have to handle this myself."

"At least, when you're getting laid, she's doing all the work. That must be nice."

I hadn't looked at my wife that way once. I felt too weak to be desirable, and I would never instigate anything after what she'd been through. I'd hardly touched her since I'd been home. When we slept together, I stuck to my side of the bed. She never talked about what she'd endured. And I never asked. I just assumed she wouldn't be ready for something like that anytime soon. I could give her all the time she needed. "It'll be a long time before Sofia and I have that sort of relationship again."

He seemed to realize how insensitive he sounded. "Of course…" He cleared his throat and took a drink. "Like I said, if there's anything you need, I'm here. My pimping duties can wait until you're back to full strength."

"Thanks." I couldn't believe my brother was sitting beside me, acting like a friend rather than a stranger. "I'm really glad you're here…and not because I need help."

It was the first time he turned his gaze away, like the statement affected him deep down inside. "Yeah…I'm glad I'm here too."

Once I was back on my feet, I moved around the house more. I showered on a daily basis, got dressed on my own, and didn't feel so weak. I started to feel like my old self, like a strong man in his prime.

Sofia stayed home with me even though I didn't need so much help anymore.

It was deep winter now, and every morning, the frost pressed against the windows. I walked around in sweatpants, but I still ditched the shirt. It just wasn't as comfortable to me. I was sitting outside on the patio because it was a sunny day. I handled work from the computer, and I only communicated with Damien through our assistants.

Sofia came outside and brought me a hot cup of coffee. "Ready for lunch?"

"Not hungry."

"You're never hungry."

All I'd been doing was lying in bed. The last thing I wanted to do was get fat. Just because I was sedentary didn't mean I could let my strength go. When I got out of this, I had to correct all my mistakes. I had to kill Maddox with my bare hands.

"You still need to eat." She took the seat beside me, wearing a long sweater dress with brown boots that went to her knees. Her brown hair was curled and long, and the makeup on her face made her seem too beautiful to be real. Her diamond ring was still on her left hand.

I had worried Maddox had taken it away. "When I'm hungry, I'll eat."

She dropped her insistence and looked at the city below her. On the outside, it seemed like nothing had changed, like she hadn't been the target of a violent crime. But there were subtle cues that I noticed. Her eyes didn't roam over my chest and shoulders the way they used to. She didn't grab the front of my shirt and yank me toward her for a kiss. When we were in bed together, she never tried to make it into something more. She didn't even try to pull me close. There was no hint of arousal in her gaze.

Maybe it was because my body was so scarred. Maybe she didn't want to hurt me. Or maybe now that I wasn't as strong as I used to be, she'd lost her lust.

Or maybe it was because of the thing I didn't want to think about.

I'd be lying if I said I didn't miss sex.

I didn't just miss it…I missed it with my wife.

I missed that closeness, that tenderness. It was the closest I could get to her heart, the closest I could get behind her walls and pretend she felt the way I did.

But I wouldn't dare pressure her. Wouldn't even mention it.

She'd have to do that on her own. Or at least tell me she was ready.

She turned her gaze back to me. "You look so much better… That makes me really happy."

"I'll be better before you know it." I never confessed how much pain I endured. I didn't tell a soul how miserable I was. I stayed positive to ease her pain. I was in this condition because I sacrificed myself for her. I didn't want her to feel worse than she already did. It was easy to focus on the finish line and forget all the roadblocks along the way.

"I know…" She reached her hand for mine on the table, her fingers so little in my palm. She gave me a gentle squeeze, accompanied by her beautiful smile.

I'd give anything to kiss her right now.

To pull her into my lap and dig my hand deep into her hair. I would love to go back to what we were before that evil man ruined our lives. It used to be just the two of us, slowly solidifying our relationship.

Now we had to start all over.

I'd earned my brother's forgiveness, but that didn't seem to matter. Now that Sofia had to struggle with this new agony, it made no difference if she could love me. She was too burdened to be able to do so anyway.

After weeks passed, I made it all the way down to the bottom floor and stepped outside. The black car was waiting for us, and I realized it was the first time I'd left the house since I came home from the hospital.

Sofia was with me, insisting she join me for my first round of physical therapy.

After we got into the back seat, the driver drove off.

She was loyal and attentive to me every moment of the day, but there was a distinct distance between us. We both had our own issues, but we refused to confide in each other. As a result, there was a minefield of silence between us.

We used to hold hands in the car, or she would rest her cheek on my shoulder. Now, we sat on opposite sides of the car, hardly saying anything to each other. When she looked out the window with a somber expression on her face, I wondered what she was thinking, if she was reliving the terrible things she never mentioned.

We arrived at the facility, and I walked inside with a straight posture, pretending to be as strong as I used to be. I didn't want Sofia to view me as weak, to assume I would never get her the revenge she deserved. I felt like I wasn't worthy of her, and I didn't want her to think that too.

Not long after we checked in at the front desk, they were ready to see me.

Sofia moved to take a seat, as if she expected to watch me until I was done.

"Sofia?"

She turned back to me, immediately enthused by the possibility of me needing her assistance. "Yes?"

"I need you to wait in the car."

Her eyes fell. She looked so hurt that it seemed like I'd slapped her across the face.

"I just need some privacy." I hated to hurt her, but I didn't want her to watch me struggle to complete ordinary tasks. It was humiliating. It wasn't a version of myself I wanted her to see.

"I don't understand…"

"I don't want you to see me like this, okay?" It was hard to deny her when her eyes looked so innocent, like she would never judge me for anything.

"See you like what?" she asked. "I don't think less of you, Hades. You could be in a wheelchair, and my opinion would never change. Watching you overcome this makes you strong, not weak. You don't have to put on a show for me. I'm your wife. I'm always gonna be here."

Her words went straight to my heart, but my pride was too great. If the therapist asked me to do something and I couldn't, I'd feel like less of a man—especially if my wife witnessed my shortcomings. If it were Ash or someone else, I probably wouldn't care. But her opinion meant the world to me. If she thought I was weak, she might never love me. "Please wait in the car." I didn't want to see the hurt look on her face, so I turned away so I wouldn't have to.

SOFIA

I SAT ACROSS FROM MY MOTHER AT THE DINNER TABLE. WE shared a bottle of wine, and I picked at the dinner Helena made for us. Fresh bread and butter were in the basket, and the room smelled like a gourmet meal.

My mother rambled on about something. "I'm so glad the Tuscan Rose seems to be operating smoothly. We've got good employees there, loyal employees. I think your father and Gustavo would be happy about this legacy. And it's amazing that Hades can keep everything tidy while going through this…"

I stared down into my glass of wine and ignored everything she said. When Hades had asked me to leave his physical therapy, I was hurt by the request. After everything we'd been through, how could he not feel comfortable with me? He'd sacrificed himself for me, did something most people wouldn't have had the courage to do. The last thing I thought was that he was weak. In fact, he had my undying respect.

I knew he probably felt guilty about what happened. But he shouldn't. In the end, he was the one who saved me.

That was all that mattered.

"He's recovering so quickly… It's remarkable. Nothing is gonna stop that man…"

Most of my dinner was untouched because I didn't have an appetite. My life was in a strange place. Time was moving so slowly, and I'd thought things would go back to the way they were, but that didn't seem possible.

We were different people.

We both struggled with our demons, and we probably would be haunted forever.

"Honey?"

I swirled my glass and took a drink.

"Sofia? Are you listening to me?"

At the mention of my name, I lifted my gaze and made eye contact with my mother. "Yes?"

She shook her head slightly. "That's a big fat no."

I didn't have the energy to entertain my mother. I didn't have the strength to smile and pretend as if everything was okay. I wanted my husband to make a full recovery and not be insecure during the process.

Her eyes softened, and she set down her glass. "Honey…we need to talk about what happened."

My mother had never provoked a conversation about what happened to me. I'd assumed she understood it was off-limits. Guess not. "No, we don't."

"It's eating you alive. I can see it."

I refused to let that asshole break me, to let him occupy my brain rent-free. If someone wronged me, I always took the classy route and brushed it off. If I kept telling myself that I was okay, maybe I would be. "What you're seeing is a woman concerned about her husband."

That look of pity continued. "Sofia, there's no shame in admitting that you aren't okay. No one would be okay."

I couldn't hold her gaze any longer, so I looked away.

My mother was an emotionless person, but right now, the pain swelled in her eyes. She couldn't hide the agony she felt at my expense, the pain a mother felt when her daughter hurt. "If you can't talk to me, talk to someone else."

"There's nothing to talk about..."

"Spending all your time pretending nothing is wrong is simply making it more wrong." She continued to stare at me hard. "Have you confided in Hades?"

He was the last person I would ever tell. "We have more important things to worry about right now. We need to get Hades back on his feet so we can resume our lives. That's the only thing that matters to me...my husband."

When the lights were out and we were ready for bed, we lay side by side in the large bed. Lights from the city pierced the crack in the curtains and were the only illumination in the darkness. I lay on my side with my back to him, but I wasn't asleep because I wasn't tired. I knew he was awake by the sound of his breathing. We weren't as close as we used to be. We managed to stay together but somehow felt like strangers. I wasn't sure if it was him or me...or both.

The mattress shifted with his movements before I felt him press his body close to mine. His chest was up against my back, and his arm hooked around my waist. His mouth rested against the back of my neck, caught in a curtain of hair. His fingertips squeezed me lightly through my t-shirt, rubbing me in the darkness.

It was the first time we were close under the sheets. He used to be too injured for closeness, but now his superficial ailments had healed. His deep breaths blanketed my skin, his warm breath hot against my skin.

I didn't hate the touch, but I didn't like it either.

Maybe my mother was right. Maybe it bothered me more than I realized.

The actual abuse I'd suffered didn't change me. It was the way I felt afterward, the way I feared people would see me. My mother looked at me like I was damaged beyond repair, and I didn't see Hades regard me with lust like he used to. He was afraid I thought he was weak. But I was afraid that he didn't feel the same way about me...that everything had changed.

That when he looked at me…all he saw was *him*.

Part of me wanted to start over, to be around someone who had no idea what had happened to me. It seemed like everyone's perception of my character had changed. That instead of being a survivor, I was a victim. I was tarnished, dirty, and irreparable.

When I projected my worst fears onto Hades, I didn't want to be near him.

Maybe he didn't want me at physical therapy because he felt differently toward me.

Maybe he'd only saved me because he felt obligated.

Maybe now he resented me for all the pain he had to carry.

I kept my eyes on the wall and gently pulled his hand off my waist. "I'm really hot right now…"

Hades stilled at my request, his entire body going rigid, but he didn't pressure me. He shifted his body away and returned to his side of the bed. This time, he turned on his side and faced the other way.

Now, we were even more distant than before.

13

HADES

I was in better shape after several sessions of physical therapy. Now I made my way around the house, taking my time up and down the stairs, but finally mobile. When I stopped by the kitchen to talk to Helena, I ran into Maria.

Initially, she'd adored me because I was a good husband for her daughter. She'd never actually cared about me, only about what I could do for her family. She practically kissed my ass like a suck-up. But now she looked at me like she genuinely cared about my well-being. "Hades, you look so good." She moved into me, very delicately, and embraced me with a gentle hug. "I'm so happy to see you moving around again."

Maybe she actually did give a damn about me. "Thank you."

"Sofia has been taking good care of you?"

She shouldn't have to. None of this should've happened in the first place. "Yes."

"She's been so worried about you. I'm glad this is almost over."

Maybe my injuries had almost healed, but my marriage was destroyed. I'd wanted my wife to fall in love with me, but now I believed that wasn't possible. I thought I'd broken the curse when I earned my brother's forgiveness, but now I wondered if that did nothing at all. Sofia and I were further apart than we'd ever been before. When I tried to hold her last night, she didn't want me to touch her. It hurt...it hurt bad. Maria stared at me like she expected me to say something, so I replied, "Yeah...we're getting there." I turned away from my mother-in-law and walked off.

Maria's voice erupted behind me. "Hades?"

I turned back around.

She came close to me, her arms over her chest with her gaze on the floor. "This is hard to say...but I'm worried about my daughter."

My heart started to beat a little harder.

"She won't talk to me about what happened. I can't get a word out of her."

The subject hit me in the chest like a wrecking ball.

Maria kept staring at me. "I know she won't see a therapist either."

The event hung over our heads like a dark cloud. It was something we all talked around, but no one mentioned specifics. We were all too disturbed to discuss it. "She hasn't mentioned it to me either." But I also never asked. I was too much of a coward to bear the burden of her story. I couldn't stand the thought of picturing what happened, of knowing exactly what he did to her.

"I think you're the only person who can talk to her. I know my daughter. She's carrying this weight inside because she thinks she can handle it on her own. But this isn't something that's just going to go away if we ignore it. Please talk to her, Hades."

She shouldn't even have to ask. That was my job, but I put myself before Sofia. Once we talked about it, it would really be real. I would have to admit that it was entirely my fault. "I will."

Maria placed her hand on my arm. "Thank you. You've always been good to her, and I appreciate it."

Whenever Sofia took a shower, she always carried her clothes into the bathroom so she could change in privacy. When she got ready for bed in the evening, she did the same thing. I hadn't seen her naked skin in over a month. It hurt that she felt the need to cover herself around me, but I tried to remember it wasn't right for me to feel anything about it.

She was in the bathroom when I decided to go out. I walked to the door and tapped my knuckles against the wood.

Sofia's voice echoed against the tile. "Yeah?"

"I'm gonna have a drink with Ash. I'll be back in an hour."

She didn't answer, but I could hear her rummaged in the bathroom as she quickly got dressed.

My own wife wouldn't let me see her naked. That wasn't good.

She opened the door a second later, a robe tied around her waist. "Where are you going?"

"The bar." I hated myself for what I'd done. I hated the fact that my own wife didn't trust me. Sometimes it made me angry, and I had to redirect that anger onto myself because it wasn't her fault. My physical injuries would heal in time, but her mental state could be permanent. It seemed like every time I came close to her, she pushed further away.

"I'm glad you feel well enough to go out."

"Yeah. It's an improvement." The only real reason I wanted to get out of the house was to take a break. I was tired of the way she looked at me—or better yet, the way she didn't look at me. "I'll see you soon." There were no more kisses on the cheek, long embraces before I walked out. Now we made exchanges like strangers.

It killed me inside.

I met Ash at the bar two minutes later. He was already seated at a table when I walked in. There were two glasses of scotch in front of him, one for him and one for me. But I suspected he got started without me long before I arrived.

I fell into the chair and immediately took a drink.

Ash leaned forward slightly, his arms resting on the table. "How are things?"

"Shitty."

"What are you talking about? I remember when you couldn't walk up the stairs. Now, here you are, walking around as a free man. That doesn't sound shitty to me."

My hand rested across the top of my glass. "I don't give a shit about my recovery. Part of me wishes I were dead."

Ash rolled his eyes. "Dramatic."

"I'm serious."

Ash didn't make another joke. "What's the problem?"

"My wife doesn't want me." As I spoke the words out loud, my chest ached in pain.

Sympathy filled his gaze.

"I love my wife more than anything in this world...and she doesn't love me back. It'll always be this way, no matter what I do. I'm doomed to suffer like this forever."

"What are you talking about?" he asked. "Of course she loves you."

I shook my head. "No. And she never will." I tilted my head back and took a drink. I set it down with a loud thud. "I know this is gonna sound crazy, but hear me out."

"You know I love crazy shit."

"When I was young, a gypsy told me I would love only one

woman…and she would never love me back. I thought it was bullshit. Who wouldn't? But everything she predicted has come true."

Ash raised an eyebrow. "You being serious right now?"

"Unfortunately."

"If that was the case, why did she marry you?"

"Because she had to."

"So, this is an arranged marriage?"

"Exactly." I took another drink. "I married her because I loved her…and she married me because she had to. I thought things would change, that we would get closer together, but after everything that has transpired, I don't think that's going to happen. She won't let me touch her. She doesn't desire me. She doesn't talk to me."

Ash ignored his drink. "If she didn't care about you, she wouldn't be at your beck and call. That woman has been deeply concerned about your well-being. Maybe she doesn't love you, but all that other stuff is untrue. She's devoted to you. I just think she has some personal shit getting in the way of that."

"And now I'll never have a chance…"

"I wouldn't say that. But it does look like you're gonna have to start over."

I rubbed my temple because this moment had already been

six years in the making. I'd worked so hard to have her, but no matter how close I got, I was never close enough.

Ash stared at me for a long time. "Go home and start over."

I lifted my gaze to meet his.

"It's time to talk about the thing you don't want to talk about."

When I came home, she was sitting in the armchair by the fire, an open book between her hands. She was in a loose t-shirt and sweatpants. Maybe she wore the extra clothes because it was wintertime, or maybe she wore them so I wouldn't see her. The woman I used to know would rather be naked because I could keep her warm.

She looked up when she noticed me. "Did you have a good time?"

No, not at all. "Yeah."

"I'm glad you got out of the house. You must feel cooped up in here."

Being in the bedroom with her all day would never suffocate me. But our distance did choke me. "We need to talk." I grabbed the book and pulled it out of her hands. I was dreading this with every beat of my heart. I was dreading this because I was a coward. I was dreading this because once her tears fell, mine would too.

She rose to her feet and tensed noticeably, her arms crossing over her chest. She didn't look like the strong woman I used to know. Now, she was timid and afraid, no longer fearless. She probably knew exactly what was coming next, and she dreaded it as much as I did.

I was always comfortable with my posture, and my hands always knew where to rest. But now I didn't know where to put them. I didn't know if I should touch her or keep them in my pockets. I didn't know if I should look her in the eye or stare at the ground. When I'd agreed to marry her, I'd agreed to the happy aspects of marriage, the newlywed phase. But I wasn't ready for the hard times, the moments that could break us forever.

She remained quiet, like she didn't know what to say.

That meant I had to rip off the bandage. "We need to talk about what happened."

She kept her eyes on the floor. "I don't want to. Just leave it alone…"

"I can't leave it alone. You won't talk with your mother about it, but that doesn't matter. You should talk to me. I'm your husband. That's what I'm supposed to do. That's my job…to help you through this."

She stayed quiet, but her breathing escalated. Clearly, she was trying to bottle her emotion, trying to pretend she was fine.

I wanted to die. "I won't make you do anything you don't want to do. If you aren't ready to talk, you don't have to. But

I want you to know that I don't see him when I look at you, that I see you as the same woman you've always been. I want you whenever you want me, and my desire for you has only grown after all this. You're still mine…I'm still yours."

She finally lifted her gaze to look at me, drops of moisture on her eyelashes. She sniffed slightly, but the tears didn't fall.

"You've been distant with me for a while now. It gets worse every passing day. The last thing I want is for us to drift further apart. We can't let this divide us. That's exactly what he wants. Please don't push me away. You get dressed in the bathroom so I can't look at you. You don't want me to touch you in bed if our embrace is anything but innocent." My eyes shifted back and forth as I looked at her face, hoping for some emotion from her. "I'll never pressure you. I'll never ask for anything you aren't ready to give. I can wait as long as you want me to…because I don't want anyone else but you. But don't push me away."

She gave a slight nod and sniffed again.

I stepped closer to her because it seemed okay. "I'm so sorry…." I took a deep breath because I felt the tears flood my eyes. Nothing could ever bring me to tears…except this one woman. I felt her pain a million times over. She thought she was alone in this, but she was never alone. Every day that she had been gone, I had still been with her…suffering. I steadied my emotion so the drops wouldn't drip down my cheeks, but the tears were visible in my eyes. "It's my fault that this happened to you…and I'll never forgive myself."

"No…it's not."

"Yes, it is. I'm the reason this happened. And I should've gotten you out sooner."

"Stop." She took a step toward me and placed her palm on my chest. "It's no one's fault. It happened, and we'll get through it." Her hands cupped my cheeks as she brought my face close to hers. Her teary eyes mirrored my own.

"We will," I whispered. "And I'll kill him. I promise you that."

She rested her forehead against mine. "I know you will."

14

SOFIA

I RETURNED TO WORK AT THE HOTEL.

Hades was nearly recovered, so he didn't need me anymore. It was nice to be back in the office, to be productive once again, but it was strange to get back to normal life.

I refused to confront the fact that I had been raped. I refused to confront the fact that I'd been a prisoner of an evil man. I tried to brush it off and pretend it didn't hurt me. But once Hades confronted me, I realized how deep those scars went. I realized Maddox was still inside me, poisoning my mind and killing my relationship. Hades was the person I trusted most in this world.

Why had I ever shut him out?

Why had I ever assumed he would think less of me?

When he said he still wanted me...I couldn't believe it. It was exactly what I needed to hear, that I hadn't been ruined by that cruel man. I needed to know that the terrible things that happened to me wouldn't change my life, especially since they were out of my control. I was a victim of a crime…and I shouldn't be punished.

I stayed in the office most of the day because my time was spent trying to catch up. It'd been months since I'd been at this desk, and the disarray showed me how much I was needed. The hotel was behind in every category. A couple employees had quit recently, and those vacancies hadn't been filled. As a result, the hotel was shorthanded, and the flow was off.

It made me realize operating this hotel completely on my own was unrealistic. If my health were compromised or one of my kids got sick, I couldn't just leave. Having a partner like Hades made everything much easier. Without him, the board would've taken over and squeezed me out.

I was looking through spreadsheets when Hades appeared in the doorway. He was in a black suit and gray tie, his expensive clothes hiding the scars and bruises underneath. His face was free of discoloration, so he looked like the handsome man he used to be. He just moved a little slower, carried his body rigidly.

I stared at him for a second, a smile slowly creeping onto my lips. "You clean up good."

His hands rested in his front pockets, and a slight look of affection was in his eyes. "I think I look better with a few scars."

"I think you look perfect no matter what."

He inched farther into my office and stopped in front of my desk. He stared at me expectantly, as if he hoped I would rise to my feet and greet him with affection. The look lasted a long time.

After our candid conversation, I felt more comfortable with him, but I wasn't ready to restart the physical relationship we had before. I'd been home for six weeks, and we hadn't kissed once. The only time I saw him naked was when I helped him get dressed.

When he realized nothing was going to happen, he prepared to turn away. "I have a meeting I should get to. I'll be back in a few hours."

I watched him turn away with guilt in my heart, and that pain made me spring to my feet and move after him. I grabbed the front of his suit and gently tugged him back toward me.

When his head turned back to me, there was already a playful smile on his lips.

I pulled him against me until our lips pressed together. It was a gentle embrace, a closed-mouth kiss that was tame. But I felt the electricity we used to share, the physical desire I'd had for him since the day we met. The chemistry was always there, no matter what we'd been through.

His body pressed into me harder, and one hand slipped beneath my hair. He cushioned the back of my neck with his fingers and deepened the kiss. His other arm circled my waist, and he brought me close to his chest. It was the way he used to kiss me, like he wasn't thinking of anyone else but me.

I tried not to think of anyone else besides my husband, but I knew that would take time. For now, it was just baby steps.

He pulled away first, his eyes on my lips like he wanted the kiss to continue. After he gave me a final squeeze, he let me go. The sense of loss was in his eyes, as if he wanted to keep kissing me and wanted to make love to me on my desk.

I probably would…if I had been ready.

To mask the sensual tension between us, I changed the subject. "Where is your meeting?"

"In the restaurant."

He never met the board there, so I wasn't sure what he was up to. "Who are you meeting?"

He didn't blink as he answered the question. "The mafia."

"You're being serious?" I knew he was telling the truth because I'd witnessed them in my hotel before. It gave me a sickly feeling, like my entire body was pierced by blades. My family's legacy had been built on a bedrock of crime. I wanted to change that, but I had no idea how.

"I never joke about the mafia."

"Why do you have to meet them in the hotel?"

"Because that's how it's always been." He could read the unease in my gaze. "You have nothing to worry about."

"I still don't like it."

"I'm sorry, but that's how it is." He headed back to the door. "I'll pick you up at the end of the day."

———

I was still at my desk when Damien walked inside. He helped himself to the chair in front of my desk. "So...is he still mad?"

Hades was in a much better mood, but I suspected that would change once Damien was mentioned. "Yes. And I don't think it's a good time to talk to him about it, if that's what you're planning on doing."

"Why?"

"Because we finally talked about...you know. The wounds are still pretty fresh."

Damien's eyes turned sad. "Are you doing okay?"

I shrugged. "I guess I feel like I have no one to talk to. It's such a terrible thing, and I don't want to hurt the people I love. Talking about it only makes them feel worse."

"You can always talk to me."

My eyes narrowed slightly.

"I can't give the best advice, but I can listen. I can hug you if that's what you need. I can tell you everything is gonna be okay and mean it."

Hades was right to be upset with Damien, but I felt bad for my husband's best friend. He was like a dog that didn't understand his misbehavior. He'd had no idea where his choices would lead, and if he had, he never would've gone through with them. He would give his life for mine in a heartbeat. "Thank you. But I think I'm okay."

"Hades was really upset about the whole thing. I won't go into the specifics."

"I know…" When I saw the tears in his eyes, I knew the depth of his heart. "Hades should be back pretty soon, so you should get going."

He sighed loudly. "The guy won't even talk to me."

"It's gonna take some time. Let the dust settle."

He bowed his head.

When I looked at the clock, I knew it was time to pack up. I'd opened my top drawer to put all my files away when I noticed the box of tampons sitting there. I didn't think twice about it at first and dropped my paperwork insides.

Damien spoke again. "We've been friends forever. I can't picture my life without him. I know things have been shit this last year, but before this, everything was fine. We've been brothers…"

"Shit."

Damien narrowed his gaze. "What?"

My thoughts went to a different place as I tried to remember the date of my last period. The last time I needed tampons, I was sitting in this office. That meant it'd been over a month since my last period. I was late...really late. My cycle was always regular, and this had never happened before. I'd been on the shot for years, and I tried to recall my last injection. I was pretty sure I'd missed my last appointment because of all the shit that was going on.

When Damien didn't get an answer, he spoke again, "Everything okay?"

"Yeah...no."

"What's wrong?"

I slammed the drawer shut and felt my heart race a million miles an hour. The truth was staring me in the face, and I wasn't ready to accept it. Being pregnant was a joyous moment, a blessing any woman would be lucky to have. In normal circumstances, I would be happy about the addition to our family, even if it was sooner than we wanted.

But who was the father?

I wasn't sure how far along I was, but it'd been over two months since I'd last been with Hades, and the rest of the time, I had been with Maddox. There was no way to know exactly when the medication wore off. Hades could've knocked me up before I was taken, or Maddox could've done it while I was his slave.

But God, I hoped it was the first.

Abortion never crossed my mind, because I would keep any baby I would ever have. Even if it was a one-night stand with a random guy, I could take care of a baby on my own. But that father of my child being a rapist...I wasn't so sure about that.

And Hades wouldn't like it either.

Just when I'd started to heal and see myself as still desirable, this happened.

This fucking freight train.

Damien continued to sit there. "Okay...you're freaking me out."

I'd forgotten he was there. "I just realized something..."

"Care to enlighten me?"

I couldn't tell him. I couldn't tell anyone. "No...I can't talk about it right now." I glanced at the clock on the wall. "You should go. He's gonna be here any..."

Hades appeared in the doorway, ice-cold at the sight of his former friend. He entered the room with a defensive posture and looked down at the man he'd marked as an enemy. His eyes were filled with loathing. Silently, he stood there.

Damien stayed in the seat and met Hades's gaze. He was apologetic, but he continued to hold his unbreakable attitude. The two men were wolves, not attacking, but always watching.

Hades was still as a statue. "Don't bother my wife."

Damien slowly got to his feet.

Even though I was overwhelmed by my news, I still fought for Damien. "He's not bothering me."

Hades didn't look at me. "Well, he's bothering me."

Damien held his gaze for a second longer, his hands resting in his pockets. "Look, I said I was sorry, and I meant it…"

Hades lost his shit right on the spot. "I don't give a fuck if you're sorry. My wife was raped, and I almost died to save her. All because you don't know how to fucking listen. I almost lost the most important thing in the world because you're like a child. I had to keep one eye on you at all times. You think an apology is gonna make Sofia forget what happened to her? What happened to me?" He started to move toward Damien, as if he was going to punch him in the mouth.

I grabbed Hades by the arm and kept him against me. "I don't blame Damien."

He yanked his arm out of my grasp. "I do. And if he doesn't get the hell out of here, I'm gonna beat him to within an inch of his life and leave him in the field where he found me."

Damien looked at Hades, watching his nostrils flare with rage. He didn't try to defend himself. He didn't try to smooth things over. He didn't even look mad at the threats. Instead, he looked heartbroken, like he was about to cry just the way Hades had cried the other night. He bowed his head and headed to the door. "I'm sorry." He stopped in the doorway and didn't turn around. "I'm sorry for everything."

15

HADES

I KNEW DAMIEN WAS SORRY.

But I didn't give a shit.

Every time I looked at him, all I could think about was what happened to my wife. What happened to me. My world crashed down around me, and instead of breaking the curse, I prolonged it.

I would suffer in this hell forever.

Damien needed to remain in my life because we needed to dispose of Maddox together. We would have to cooperate and collaborate if we hoped to achieve that. Putting aside our differences seemed easy in theory. But in real life, it was impossible.

I took Sofia home, and we sat in silence in the back seat. She had been calmer around me before, and we'd even shared a spectacular kiss in her office. But all that magic had been wiped away after Damien emerged. I tried not to let his presence spoil that small victory, but it was difficult.

Normally, Sofia would tell me that I was being too harsh with Damien, that I needed to calm down and forgive him. But now, she looked out the window, so quiet it was like I wasn't even there. Like that kiss never happened…or at least, it seemed that way.

We returned to the house and entered our bedroom. Sofia immediately walked into the bathroom, and a moment later, I heard the water running to fill that bath. The door remained closed, and she didn't come out for several hours.

I sat on the balcony in the freezing cold air, my expensive suit still on, and I thought about how Sofia's attitude had completely flipped. She judged me for my cruelty, but she had no idea how hurt I was. My best friend fucking betrayed me. It wasn't intentional, but it was still a betrayal nonetheless.

How could she think less of me?

My relationship with Damien was none of her business. Just as her relationship with her mother was none of mine.

I stewed in my anger for hours, unaffected by the cold air. I never got sick, so that wasn't a concern. I needed the cold temperature to freeze the rage in my temples. Sometimes I wondered if I put the blame on Damien so I wouldn't have to feel the burden myself. She was my wife, so I was responsible too.

But I was too traumatized to accept that fact.

It was easier to blame him.

I wanted to storm into the bathroom and demand her affection, like she could just turn it on with the press of a button. I was frustrated because I wanted her so much—not just physically, but emotionally. I'd gotten a taste of it when she grabbed the front of my suit and pulled me in for a kiss.

It was the most healing I had received in a month.

It was like a warm fire that thawed my bones. Once that blaze was extinguished, I was frozen once again. And miserable. And bitter.

As if that kiss had never happened, she was cold once again.

She only got dressed in the bathroom, and we didn't snuggle in bed. The most affection I got from her was the occasional hug. But it was like hugging your aunt…no heat. It was practically obligatory.

What the fuck was I going to do?

A week went by, and our relationship didn't improve. It was on a steady decline, getting worse and worse. I went to her office to pick her up at the end of the day, but I wasn't sure if I could keep my rage bottled deep inside. I was angry with her, when I had no right to be. I was asking for something she couldn't give.

But when I walked inside and saw the way she hardly looked at me, I snapped. "Look at me." I stood in front of her desk and looked down at her, my hands in my pockets. I watched the way she looked over her paperwork like that was more important than I would ever be. I'd asked her not to shut me out, but she did it anyway. Now she was doing it worse than before. My voice didn't rise, but its potency made the walls vibrate. I wasn't angry at her...just angry with this ghost version of her.

She lifted her gaze and met my eyes, her entire body rigid with unease. That hostile fire wasn't in her eyes like it used to be.

"Put that shit down and stand up." I hadn't spoken to her like this in a long time, but my patience had officially expired. "When your husband walks in the door, you give him your full attention. You hug him, you kiss him, and you make him feel like a king. I always treat you like a queen, and I demand that same respect."

She slowly rose to her feet and looked extremely timid.

"I thought we'd made progress after our last conversation, but then I screamed at Damien, and you shut off. I know you suffered in ways I can never understand, but I suffered too. I took a beating that nearly killed me, and I don't regret it because it gave me you. But I have emotional scars that I am carrying, and I need you to comfort me. This is a two-way street. This is a marriage. We need to be there for each other. So, stop treating me like I don't matter. Treat me like your husband."

Emotion welled in her eyes, but she didn't form tears. Her arms crossed over her chest, and her gaze drifted down to the floor. Her right hand rubbed her left arm absentmindedly, like she was comforting herself under my stare.

"I told you to look at me."

She lifted her chin once again and took a deep breath. "I'm sorry... I'm just stressed out right now."

"I'm stressed out too. But that doesn't stop me from loving..." I controlled my response before it turned into something I would regret. "It doesn't stop me from being a husband to you."

Her eyes shifted back and forth as she looked into mine. She didn't seem to understand what I had been about to say, that I was about to tell her how much I loved her.

"This is the hand we've been dealt. We need to work to make it better. Shutting down and ignoring each other is not the solution. Working our asses off is a solution. You need to meet me halfway here."

She tightened her arms around her body. "I know..."

"Then be better."

She dropped her gaze.

"Unless there's something you're not telling me."

She looked at the floor a moment longer before she lifted her chin to meet my look. There was no confidence in her eyes, just a look of fear. She responded with an answer that contradicted her expression. "No."

She wouldn't lie to me, so I let it go. "Then get your ass over here and kiss me."

There was a pause of several seconds before she obeyed. She slowly moved around the desk before she walked up to me. She stopped when there was a foot between us, like she needed some space before she could give me what I wanted.

"I'm not asking for more than what you can give. I just want you..." I would never demand her to strip off her clothes and get into bed. I would never force her to rush into a physical relationship if she wasn't ready. But I needed her affection, needed to know that we still had each other.

"Hades, it's not you..."

"Sometimes it feels like it is."

"It's not... I promise. I just..."

"What?"

She took a long time to answer. "I'm just overwhelmed, I guess."

"You don't need to feel overwhelmed with me. Whatever happens out there doesn't affect what happens with us. This relationship is for life. There is nothing in this world that will ever divide us. When I married you, I pledged my loyalty, my lifelong commitment, my devotion. Nothing will break that. Ever."

Her eyes shone with emotion before they tilted to the ground.

My fingers moved under her chin, and I lifted her gaze. "Nothing."

She slowly moved into my chest and rested her forehead against my hard body. She took a deep breath when she felt me, like she was letting the stress evaporate from her skin.

My arms wrapped around her waist, and I pulled her close to me, holding her like she needed this as much as I did. I smelled her hair, felt her beautiful curves, held my wife like a man madly in love.

She must know I loved her...because it was so fucking obvious.

It was so obvious that I was desperately, stupidly, ridiculously in love with my wife.

16

SOFIA

THE HOTEL WAS THE ONLY PLACE I HAD PRIVACY, SO I SAT ON the toilet in the bathroom with the stick in my hand. I held it between my fingers and stared at the results.

Pregnant.

I wasn't shocked by the results because I already knew that's what it would say. I hadn't had a period in almost two months. Since I was so regular, that just wasn't normal. I wasn't some scared teenager who wasn't ready to be a mother. I was a grown-ass woman who wanted a family.

Just not like this.

I had no idea who the father was. I'd slept with Hades the night before I was captured, so maybe that was the moment I conceived. But it easily could've happened when I was a prisoner of Maddox.

No way to know.

What would Hades say when I told him? Just when we tried to move past what happened, this curve ball was thrown our way. We could've moved on, but now that there was a baby in the mix, we would always be reminded of what happened.

We wouldn't survive that.

When Hades told me he was committed to me forever, I almost told him the truth. But I knew he wouldn't be as supportive if he knew I was pregnant by the man who'd raped me. He'd be disgusted, probably ask me to get an abortion.

I'd considered the idea too, but I couldn't go through with it.

Even if I did a DNA test to conclude it did belong to Maddox...I still wasn't sure. If that happened, would Hades force me to do it anyway? He didn't have the same sense of morals as I did. To him, everything was black and white. He'd killed people before. He wouldn't lose any sleep over this.

But if I kept the baby, he might leave me.

I wished there were a way to know who the baby belonged to before I approached him with the news. I couldn't keep this secret forever. He always saw me fully clothed now, but eventually, he would start to notice the changes in my body. He was too smart to be fooled.

I clutched the stick in my hand and closed my eyes for a moment. The one person I wanted to turn to was the person I couldn't confide in. He was my best friend…but now he was a stranger.

I hadn't wanted to marry him in the first place, but now I couldn't picture my life without him. I wouldn't know what to do if I lost him. The man had become everything to me. He didn't look at me differently after what happened, and that made me realize how good of a man he was.

Made me realize how lucky I was to be married to him.

But maybe all of that would change when he knew the truth.

I grabbed my phone and made the call.

Damien picked up right away. "Sofia, everything okay?"

He asked the question because I never called. "Can you meet me in fifteen minutes?"

We met at a restaurant across the street from the hotel. I took a gamble leaving the property because Hades was in and out of the hotel throughout the day. Once he realized I was gone, he'd want to know where I was.

If I told him I was with Damien, I could lie and say I was comforting him about their relationship. It was believable.

Damien and I didn't order anything because neither one of us was hungry. We just needed a place to talk. The waitress kept bugging us, so Damien ordered us a couple of drinks and an appetizer just to get her off our back. Now we had two glasses of wine, but I didn't take a drink because I couldn't.

Damien gave me his full attention. He was tense at the table, his shoulders rigid and his hands balled tightly into fists. He'd already asked me what was wrong three times, and since I never gave an answer, he decided to be quiet.

"I need to tell you something... I don't know who else to talk to."

"I doubt I can be much help, but I'm always here for you."

"You know Hades the best, so you're my best option."

His eyes narrowed.

"You have to promise me you won't tell him what I'm about to tell you."

Now he looked even more uncomfortable. He took a deep breath and sighed audibly. He grabbed his glass and took a deep drink, handling it like scotch instead of wine. "You're putting me in a tough spot. I'm already in the doghouse."

"I understand that, but I have nowhere else to go."

He sighed again. "Okay, you're scaring me."

"I'm scared too."

He leaned forward and rested his hands against his lips. He stared at me for a long time before he dropped his hands back to the table. "If he finds out I kept a big secret from him, I'll really have no chance of fixing anything. It'll be the final nail in the coffin."

"I know I'm asking for a lot. I don't know what else to do."

"Talk to him. You can talk to him about anything."

"Not about this…"

He rubbed the back of his neck before he finally gave in. "Okay, I'm all ears."

It would be the first time I would admit the truth out loud. It was scary, like jumping out of a plane to skydive. "I'm pregnant."

His body tensed noticeably but relaxed an instant later. He sighed in relief before his eyes softened. "There's nothing to be afraid of. Hades will be very happy. Track him down and tell him. He'll be over the moon."

If I'd gotten pregnant sooner than we'd planned, he wouldn't have cared. He would've been supportive and excited. He was the kind of man that wasn't afraid of a challenge, wasn't afraid of the unexpected. But that wasn't the situation now. "I'm not sure if he's the father."

The color drained from Damien's face, and he began to look sick. His hands covered his face, and he sighed quietly to himself. His fingers dug into his hair, and he groaned in misery. After a moment, he dropped his hands and looked at me. "Shit."

"Yeah…"

"And you have no idea…?"

I answered his unspoken question. "No. Not unless I get a paternity test."

"Fuck. I'm so sorry."

I nodded slightly and battled the emotion in my throat. It should be a happy moment for me, but it was one of the worst in my life. "I'm afraid to tell him the truth. He'll either ask me to get an abortion…or he'll leave. Our relationship is already rocky as it is. Now, this…" I held on to the stem of my wineglass even though I couldn't take a drink. "I've loved being married to him. I didn't expect that to happen, but it did. The last thing I want is to lose him…"

Damien was quiet as he plotted a response. "I'm not sure what he's going to say. I'm not going to lie—he's not going to be happy about this, about the fact that this is happening to you at all. But I can promise you he's gonna stick by your side, no matter what. He would never force you to do anything you didn't want to do. That man will be just as committed to you as he ever was. Tell him."

"I don't see how he could look past this…" My eyes shifted to the table. "If the baby isn't his, he's not going to want anything to do with it. He's not going to want anything to do with me. The baby needs to be his, or I need to get an abortion."

Damien shook his head. "No."

"What do you mean, no?"

"Hades would never react that way."

"Why wouldn't he? This isn't what he signed up for. He's not going to want to be burdened with raising a kid from another man. It doesn't make any sense for him to be accommodating."

Damien looked across the restaurant, several thoughts dancing across the surface of his eyes. He was quiet for a long time, thinking to himself. He eventually shook his head slightly. "I just do. I know how he feels about you."

"I know I'm his wife, but this is more complicated than that."

He closed his eyes for a moment as if he were restraining himself. "Just tell him, Sofia."

I never considered myself to be a coward.

I'd always been fearless, never afraid of anyone else. Outside opinions and thoughts never dictated my feelings. But then again, I'd never cared about someone the way I cared about Hades. His opinion meant the world to me.

It meant everything.

So I continued to keep the truth bottled inside because I was scared.

I got ready for bed in the bathroom, changing into a long t-shirt that hid the curves of my body from view. When I rubbed my palm over my stomach, I noticed the little bulge that had started to form. I'd noticed it before, but I'd assumed I'd just been gaining weight. I'd been at home taking care of Hades, so all I ever did was eat and sit.

Now I realized it wasn't extra weight. It was a new person.

After I washed my face and brushed my teeth, I returned to the bedroom and got under the covers.

Hades was already in bed, the sheets resting over his hips. He was shirtless, his strong pecs reflecting the light from the slightly open window. The scars and bruises had faded, so his beautiful tanned skin was visible once more. He was a handsome man; that couldn't be denied. It wasn't like I was oblivious to it.

I just wasn't ready.

I pulled the sheets to my shoulders and closed my eyes.

Hades immediately shifted closer to me. He positioned himself right in front of me, just inches between us. He didn't touch me, as if he was waiting for permission.

I opened my eyes and saw his face directly next to mine. I knew what he wanted from me, noticed the way he was hard for me in his sweatpants. I knew he wanted my affection, even just a simple touch. I might have been okay with it, but then I found out I was pregnant, and the last thing I wanted was to be intimate.

It seemed like Hades meant what he said, that he still desired me as much as he had before.

Hades wrapped his arm around my waist and pulled us closer together. He grabbed my thigh and hooked it over his hip. We used to sleep this way all the time. I would wake up in the same position, my hand resting against his chest. The outline of his cock was noticeable, pressed right against me. He probably didn't mean to make it obvious, but it was impossible to hide. "Baby." His husky voice pierced the darkness, filled with longing and desire. He moved his forehead against mine, as if he wanted to kiss me. His hand slipped underneath my t-shirt and slid up my back. "I miss you."

"I know… I'm just not ready."

"That's not what I mean. I miss this…us." He pressed his lips to mine and gave me a gentle kiss. He tested my response by keeping it slow, delicate. His mouth remained closed. He kissed me again, his lips moving to the corner of my mouth.

I enjoyed being the recipient of his affection, being the only woman in his bed. But I felt so scared, so uneasy about the secret I was keeping from him that I couldn't do it. If we slept together and he didn't realize I was pregnant with potentially another man's child, it would feel so deceitful. It made me feel like a liar, made me feel ugly. I kissed him back so I didn't reject him outright, but then I pulled away.

If he was disappointed, he didn't let me see it. He rested his forehead against mine and closed his eyes. "Goodnight, baby."

"Goodnight…"

I knew I was having a dream. But I couldn't force myself to wake up.

I knew it wasn't real, but I was still scared. Terrified.

Maddox was on top of me, his possessive gaze locked on mine. We were naked together, and he was using my body like he owned it. One hand was on my neck, and he choked me while he fucked me.

I threw my hands in his face to fight him off. There was so much hatred in my body, and it was about to explode. I hated him so much, hated him enough to kill him with my bare hands. "Die, motherfucker." I swung my arms around, striking him in the face, in the chest.

"Sofia."

I screamed as I fought, fought for my life.

"Sofia." Large hands grabbed my arms and shook me gently. "Baby, wake up."

"I'm gonna kill you." Hot tears poured down my face as I kept fighting.

"Come on." He shook me again.

My eyes opened and focused on the shadow on top of me, the outline of a man. His face wasn't visible because it was too dark, but his physique was thick and powerful. Faceless, he was terrifying.

Maybe it wasn't a dream. "Get off me." I tried to slam my hands into his face, but he restrained me on the bed.

"Baby, it's me. Hades."

"I can't see your face…" I continued to squirm in his grasp.

He leaned down closer to me so our faces were practically touching. "It's me. Listen to my voice."

When I saw his brown eyes and realized they weren't blue, I knew Maddox wasn't on top of me. I knew I was in bed at home, waking up from a terrible nightmare. None of it was real. Just a horrible flashback that my subconscious brain was trying to confront. I took a deep breath and felt my muscles relax.

When Hades knew I was calm, he let me go. He moved off me and gave me some space. "Just a dream."

I sat up and blinked a couple times. The sight of the bedroom came to me, and I listened to my breathing start to slow. I turned my gaze on him and noticed the concern in his eyes. That was when I noticed the blood coming from his nose. "Oh no, I'm so sorry." I reached my hand out to wipe the blood away with my fingers.

He grabbed my wrist and pulled it away from his face so I wouldn't touch it. "I'm fine. Don't worry about it." He gently guided my hand back to the bed. "I'm sorry you had a nightmare." He didn't ask what it was about, probably because he could figure it out.

I leaned against the headboard and pulled my knees to my

chest. The nightmare was still fresh in my brain. I could feel the tightness around my throat from where he had grabbed me, could feel the penetration between my legs even though he hadn't been there. My arms folded over my chest, and I cradled myself.

Hades cleaned up his nose in the bathroom then returned to me. He sat beside me against the headboard and grabbed my hand. He interlocked our fingers and gave me a gentle squeeze. "It's gonna be okay. I promise."

No, it wasn't going to be okay. Reality came flooding back to me, and I remembered I was pregnant and, knowing my luck, that psychopath was the father. He would always have a hold on me, always have ownership over me. My heart started to race, and I panicked all over again. My husband was the one person who could comfort me.

What if I lost him?

What if he left me?

What would I do without him?

I'd never wanted to get married because I didn't believe in marriage, monogamy, and trust. But I got all those things with Hades. I got a good man whom I respected and admired, who took care of me and would do anything to keep me safe. I'd initially wanted to be single, but now that was the last thing I wanted.

I wanted to be Mrs. Lombardi forever.

New tears started to escape my eyes.

"Baby…it was just a dream." He wrapped his arms around my shoulders and brought me closer to his chest. His lips moved to my forehead, and he gave me a gentle kiss. "Shh… it'll be alright. I am here with you…and I'll always be here with you."

17

HADES

I WAITED AT THE BAR WITH A DRINK IN MY HAND.

It was late, sometime between eleven and twelve. Other than a couple talking in the corner, I was the only one there. In jeans and a dark jacket, I sat alone and glanced at the time on my watch. I didn't want to have this meeting, but I had no choice.

Watching Sofia writhe in a painful dream showed me how tortured, how disturbed she truly was. I suspected Maddox did even worse things than what I imagined. He'd hurt my wife so deeply.

I would hurt him even more.

I wanted to encourage her to see a therapist, but that made it seem like I didn't want to talk to her about it. In truth, I didn't. I wouldn't be able to keep a straight face as she described such horrible things. I would either punch down a wall or burst into tears.

Neither was good.

Maybe killing Maddox would give her the closure she needed. I certainly needed it.

The door opened, and Damien walked inside. He was dressed as casually as I was, but there was a hint of threat to his frame. It was something I could easily recognize because I saw it in myself.

He made eye contact with me and joined me at the bar. His knuckles tapped against the bar, and he ordered a scotch from the guy waiting on us. Soon, there was a fresh glass in front of us, and we were both ready to drink our pain away.

The tension was palpable. My hatred was obvious, and it seemed to bounce off Damien and hit me right in the face. It was like looking in a mirror, and I could feel my own hatred absorb into my skin.

Damien looked straight ahead and didn't meet my gaze. It didn't seem like he wanted to be there either. He slid the glass on the surface, watching the contents swirl around.

I didn't know what to say. I was too angry to get words out.

Damien cleared his throat. "How's Sofia?"

"She's been worse. She's also been better."

"That didn't really answer my question."

I lost my temper. "My wife was raped. How do you think she is?"

Damien sighed quietly, his eyes still on his drink. "She'll get through this… Give it time."

"Easy for you to say. You don't have to see her every day. She woke up last night having a nightmare…and I know exactly what her nightmare was about."

Damien drank from his glass then slouched forward. "Maybe she should see a therapist."

I stared at the side of his face and didn't answer.

"Then we need to focus on killing Maddox. You seem well enough."

I stared at the mirror on the wall, seeing the two of us sitting together, plotting the death of our greatest enemy. "I couldn't agree more. But I don't know where to start. He's impossible to find."

"Then we'll make it possible. I want to kill this fucker as much as you do."

No. No one wanted to kill him as much as I did. "If we can't hunt him down, then we need to lure him out." But that was easier said than done. He had his henchmen to do all his dirty work. He only poked his head out when he wanted to have a good time. "The only way to smoke him out is to affect his business. Get his drugs off the street. Force him to confront us, since he has no other option."

Damien gave a slight nod. "That's not a bad idea. It'll take time…but it'll happen."

"We can find his distributors and kill them. Without those

men, he has no way to get his drugs on the streets. We know enough people, we have enough connections, we should be able to pull it off."

Damien tapped his glass against the surface, getting the guy's attention.

The bartender refilled Damien's glass. When he tried to fill mine, I simply shook my head.

I couldn't drink the way I used to.

Damien took a drink, then turned in his chair to face me. Now that we were talking about something bigger than the two of us, it started to feel like old times, it started to feel like us. "The guy takes things personally. And he'll personally come after us. He'll definitely be pissed off."

"Good. I want him to be pissed off."

"Are you sure you're ready for that? I mean, you haven't recovered all the way yet."

It would take a long time to be back to normal, but I was well enough to do what needed to be done. "I'm ready."

Damien stared at me for a while, as if he were reading my gaze. He didn't object to what I said, just let it be. "Then we'll start as soon as possible. No going back."

I didn't want to go back. I wanted to finish this. I wanted to do what I should've done a long time ago. "Then we're done here." I rose to my feet and prepared to depart.

Damien grabbed my arm. "Hang on."

I twisted out of his hold and gave him a venomous stare. "Don't touch me again."

Damien returned his hand to his thigh. He looked at me for a while, apology slowly coming into his gaze. "I don't want it to be this way. Hades, you mean the world to me. I would die for you...I mean that. I love Sofia like a sister, and I hate myself for what happened to her. I just want you to know that."

I stared at him for several seconds, and I almost felt the sympathy in my heart. But it disappeared quickly, evaporating like boiling water. I turned my gaze away and walked off, leaving him alone at the bar.

When I walked in the door, it was past midnight. I gently shut the bedroom door behind me so Sofia wouldn't wake. It was dark because all the lights were off, so I slowly crept to my closet and undressed.

When I walked back to the bed, I realized she was awake.

Wide awake.

I stopped at the edge of the bed and looked at her, seeing her expressive eyes. She didn't look tired at all. Instead, she looked exhausted but unable to sleep.

She stared at me with unblinking eyes. "Where were you?"

"Out with Damien." I pulled the sheets back and got into bed.

She seemed uncomfortable with that answer. "With Damien at this time of night?"

Did she not believe me? Why was that so hard to believe? "Yes."

She turned her gaze away, visibly closing herself off from me.

I leaned against the headboard and stared at the side of her face. "I'm missing something."

She looked out the patio doors even though the view was blocked by the closed curtains.

When she didn't say anything, I pressed further. "Talk to me."

She refused to look at me.

"Don't make me ask you again."

She slowly turned her gaze my way, her eyes reflecting the sliver of light in the bedroom. "Don't lie to me."

My heart started to slam in my chest. My initial response was anger.

No. It was rage.

I was an honest man, so honest, it got me into deep shit all the time. And the idea that I would lie to her, my own fucking wife, was bullshit. I had to carefully swallow those emotions and not explode at her. "I'm not lying."

"You hate Damien. And you have no reason to talk to him in the middle of the night." She looked forward once again.

I had to take a couple breaths so I wouldn't do something stupid. "And what do you think I was doing?"

"You already know."

I reminded myself of everything she'd been through…due to my mistakes. I reminded myself that she was emotionally stunted. I remembered her view of marriage before she became my wife. All she'd ever known was rich men with mistresses. Now that our relationship was rocky, she assumed the worst. If only she knew how much I loved her, she would understand how fucking stupid she sounded. I wanted to tell her then and there that I was madly in love with her. I'd rather spend a lifetime with her not getting laid than spend my nights with endless beautiful women. "I'm gonna cut you some slack, 'cause shit is hard right now. Let me remind you that I'm painfully honest. If I'm fucking someone, I'll say it to your face. Spoiler alert. I'm not. If I tell you something, it's the complete truth. I was with Damien at the bar talking about Maddox."

She wouldn't look at me.

"When I told you I was committed to this marriage, I meant it. Just because we aren't having sex doesn't mean I'm gonna go looking for it somewhere else. You're the only woman I want… I wish you understood that. The only reason I'm not screaming at you right now is because I know you've been through a lot. But I would never do that, no matter how hard things get. You could never sleep with me again, and

I'd still be right here. I'm in this for the long haul. Even if you wanted to divorce me, I wouldn't let you. It's you and me...forever. Do you understand that?"

Her breathing picked up noticeably, and she turned her head slightly farther to the right so I couldn't see her face. She was unresponsive to my declaration, but her heightened breathing relayed its own story.

"Sofia, do you understand that?"

She ignored me.

My voice became sterner. "Look at me. Now."

She fought me initially, but when her body started to shake, it was obvious she'd lost the battle. She finally turned her face back to me, eyes full of tears and with wet cheeks. Her bottom lip was trembling because she couldn't keep her emotions stable.

It broke my heart to see her like that, to see such a strong woman feel so insecure. If she only understood the depth of my feelings, she would understand just how perfect she was, regardless of the things that had happened to her. But it also told me she was scared to lose me, that she didn't want me to be with anyone else, that she wanted me all to herself. She was invested in this marriage, and her guard was down. That meant I could hurt her...and that terrified her.

"Baby, I'm yours." I moved into her side and wrapped my arms around her. I brought her close and cradled her face against my chest. My fingers slid into the back of her hair, and I held her against me. I listened to my wife cry, listened to her open her heart to me. She underappreciated her value and thought I would do the same thing. "I will never hurt you. I promise."

Her arm wrapped around my waist, and she cuddled into me. Her tears only lasted a few more minutes before she forced herself to calm down. Once the silence was the only sound between us, she whispered into the darkness, "I don't want to lose you."

Those words brought me joy, but they also brought me pain. My chin rested on her head so she couldn't see my face. She couldn't see the moisture that built up in my eyes. "You could never lose me."

Our relationship improved over the week.

She wasn't as distant with me. She extended affection often, kissing me goodbye when I dropped her off at work and embracing me when I picked her up again. When we went to sleep together, our bodies were always wrapped around each other.

But it never went further than that.

I noticed she still didn't change in front of me. Her outfit changes always took place in the bathroom. It was strange because I'd never given her the impression that I'd tear her clothes off and bend her over the bed. I was always delicate now, and I would never pressure her unless she explicitly told me that was what she wanted. So changing in the bathroom seemed a little excessive.

But I didn't dare complain.

I was in my office at the bank when Damien walked inside. Unfortunately, we had to deal with each other often. It was always uncomfortable, always tense. But we usually said whatever needed to be said and went on about our day.

Damien approached my desk, his eyes guarded and his hands in the pockets of his suit. "How's Sofia?"

I noticed he only asked about her. He hardly asked about me. "Better."

He gave a slight nod. "Good."

I was still used to telling him everything, so I wanted to tell him what Sofia had accused me of last week. She actually thought I was sneaking around behind her back. She actually thought I went to a whorehouse or picked up a woman at a bar. It was ludicrous, because I would never find a woman who compared to her.

When we had nothing else to say, Damien spoke. "I got a good list of his distributors. I sent the guys out to take care of it, but it'll be a while before we get them all."

"I'm available if we need more hands on deck."

"I'm already getting my hands dirty. I think you should stay home with Sofia. She needs you right now."

That was a valid point. When I was gone just one night, she

assumed I was having an affair. She probably couldn't sleep unless I was there. I didn't know what her sleeping arrangements had been with Maddox, if she had been forced to sleep beside him every night. I suspected that wasn't the case because Sofia would've killed him with her bare hands. "True."

"The guy doesn't have a single person he cares about. Just drugs and money. Doesn't even hit up the whorehouses. The only person he has some kind of vested interest in is you. If that weren't true, he would've killed you."

"So, if he knows I am the one who's compromising his livelihood, he'll probably be provoked."

Damien nodded. "Yeah. Who knows what he'll do. He might even knock on your front door."

Maddox was definitely unpredictable.

"Ash offered to help." Damien pulled his hands out of his pockets and crossed his arms over his chest. "It's crazy to think he hated you, and now he's doing everything he can to help you." He stared at me like he expected me to say something to that.

"What are you trying to say?"

He shook his head. "Things change…"

SOFIA

I was in my office when Damien stopped by.

He didn't verbally announce his presence. He just stepped inside, dressed casually in jeans and a sweater. He helped himself to the chair in front of my desk.

I closed my laptop so nothing obstructed my view.

He stared at me with wide eyes for several seconds. "You need to tell him."

Guilt washed over me. Several weeks had gone by, and I was getting bigger and bigger. It was a miracle Hades hadn't figured it out by now. Maybe he just assumed I was gaining weight and didn't dare act like he noticed.

"Sofia, it's been long enough."

"I know…"

"The longer you wait, the more he's going to be blindsided.

And if you decide you don't want to keep the baby, you're running out of time for that too."

"That's not an option." I was aware of the life living inside me, the little person developing in my womb. This was a real entity to me, and I could never live with the guilt of taking its life away. If I really didn't want to raise the baby, I could give it up for adoption. But I didn't think I could even do that.

"Either way, he deserves to know. This is your husband we're talking about. That man has been nothing but good to you, and it's ridiculous to think that would ever change. I know you've been through a lot, but his feelings are no different than they used to be."

For the last few months, I'd felt uneasy. I wasn't sure where I belonged, if my value had changed. My emotional instability prevented me from reading the truth right in front of me. Hades hadn't changed...I had.

But this was totally different.

I was still afraid he would leave once he knew the truth.

And I couldn't blame him if he did.

Damien continued to watch me. "I've kept your secret, but I can't do it much longer. When I look him in the eye, I feel like a traitor for not telling him this. It needs to come from you. So, do it soon."

I had been dragging my feet because I knew it would change everything. I didn't want to accept my fate, accept my future. Would we survive what was about to come? I was already afraid Hades would walk out at any moment.

"Don't be scared."

"You have no idea what I'm going through..."

"No," he said. "But I know your husband better than you do."

Damien's words pierced my conscience. Whether Hades was the father or not, he deserved to know what was going on. He wasn't just a man I was seeing. He was a man I'd pledged a lifetime to. What happened to me happened to him.

It was too cold to sit outside on the terrace, so we sat at the table inside. We finished a great meal Helena had prepared for us. There was always a basket of fresh bread, and I ate more of it than I usually did.

Because now I was eating for two.

Wine was always poured, but I never drank from my glass. Thankfully, Hades didn't seem to notice.

Our dinner was spent mostly in silence. We were closer than we had been before, but not back to normal. There was a distinct distance between us, like we each had our own secrets. Now was the right time to tell him...but I didn't want to.

It would change everything.

It would make this real.

In a couple months, I would be a mother. And I had no idea who the father of my child was.

I took a deep breath, and when I finally found the courage to come clean, he spoke instead.

"Damien and I are working on Maddox." It didn't matter if it was deep winter, he preferred his shirtless attire, his sweatpants that were low on his hips. He wasn't back to weight training or his previous exercise regimen, but he was still strong. His chest muscles were like two slabs of concrete, and his stomach was so tight you could grate cheese on it.

The mention of my greatest enemy made me forget what I was about to tell him. "What does that mean?"

"It means we decided to hit him where it hurts...his business. That seems to be the only thing he cares about. We are going after his distributors, the guys on the ground that sell his drugs on the streets. He has bigger partners that ship his product to the rest of Europe. I'm taking those guys out too."

That sounds like serious business. "That sounds like war..."

He wore a brooding gaze, like he could snap at any moment. During quiet moments, he seemed to be the angriest. He probably relived the terrible things we both endured, and it pissed him off all over again. His eyes returned to mine. "It is war."

War meant there was a battle on two sides. Someone had to lose. I just hoped it wasn't us. "Couldn't you just track him down and kill him? He's gotta live somewhere, right?"

He shook his head slightly. "The guy is never in the same place for long. And he doesn't have allies...he doesn't let anyone in. So I can't torture anyone for answers."

"Could I lure him out?" Of course, I didn't want to be the bait. I never wanted to see that man again. Just looking at him would make me shake. But my desire to kill him outweighed my fear. I was willing to do anything to see him dead, even risk myself in the process. It wasn't just vengeance for what he did to me. But for what he did to my husband.

Hades's eyes narrowed on my face, and his eyebrows furrowed. There was a hint of rage in the look, like he was about to tell me off. But he wrested control of his emotions and let it go. "No."

"It might be easier that way."

"I said no."

I didn't press further because it was like poking an angry bear. If I pressed my stick into his side too many times, he would eventually turn on me and maul me to death. The quiet companionship we'd had minutes ago was long gone. The only thing left to do was the one thing I didn't want to.

So I didn't.

I couldn't drag my feet any longer, so I took myself to the doctor. If I were going to keep this baby, I needed to make sure everything was okay, that I grabbed my prenatal vitamins and did everything I could to prepare for how my life would change.

I never had been afraid to do anything alone before Hades came into my life. But now it felt so strange to be by myself. He should be there with me, holding my hand and telling me everything would be okay.

But even if he knew the truth, would he say those things?

Maddox was a man he hated more than anyone. Could Hades realistically accept this child if it weren't his? Would he be a supportive husband? Or would he turn me away for good? He said he would always be there…but he had no idea what was coming next.

The doctor gave me the news I'd been waiting for.

I was almost four months along. That meant it was possible the baby could belong to Hades. But it was equally possible that it didn't. The doctor also said he could tell me the gender of the baby.

But I didn't want to know. My husband didn't even know I was pregnant. I didn't want to get that far ahead. But at least the baby was healthy.

That was something to be thankful for.

I was in my office when Hades came by. Instead of waiting for me to stand and greet him, he lowered himself into the chair and rested one ankle on the opposite knee. His hands came together, and he stared at me with wide-open eyes.

My skin turned cold. I didn't like that look. He never stared at me that way…like I was his enemy. I could tell he was angry, could feel it in the air around us. It made my heart race painfully, made my skin turn warm.

Hades kept up his stare and said nothing.

I shut my laptop and put my stuff away. "I'm ready to go."

He continued to sit there. "Where were you?"

I froze on the spot.

His malicious eyes stayed glued to my face. "I came by, and you weren't here. No one could tell me where you'd gone."

"Why didn't you just call?"

His eyes narrowed. "Why don't you just answer my question?"

I grabbed my purse and tried to breathe through the suffocation. "I had a personal errand."

"What kind of errand?"

I started to lose my temper. "You don't tell me every little thing you do."

He rose to his feet. "Because I can take care of myself. How can I protect you when I don't know where you are?"

"You said I had nothing to worry about."

He stared at me for a while, like he didn't have a rebuttal.

"It was personal. Just leave it alone."

His anger died away, and his eyes slowly softened. He probably understood how much he was cornering me, how uncomfortable he was making me. "You can tell me anything. How many times do I have to say that?"

"I will tell you. I'm just not ready."

Whenever we were home, the only space I got was in the bathroom. If I visited the rest of the house, I would run into my mother. She was nosier than he was, so she wouldn't get off my case.

I stood in the shower under the warm water. My hair stuck to the back of my neck, and my hand grazed over my slightly extended stomach. Now I could really feel the person inside me. It wasn't that obvious, but I was so thin that any weight gain was noticeable. But this wasn't general weight gain. It was all concentrated in one spot. If someone saw me in just my underwear, they would assume I was in the early stages of pregnancy.

I closed my eyes and tried to relax. I could just pretend the baby belonged to Hades, and that would help me be happy. I could keep lying until I believed it. But if the baby came out with blue eyes and similar features to Maddox, I would have to lie every moment of every day to convince myself otherwise.

I was deep in thought when I noticed the slight click of the door behind me. My eyes snapped open, and my body turned rigid when I realized I wasn't alone. I wasn't afraid to be naked with my husband because he would never pressure me into something I wasn't ready for. But now that I was buck naked, my belly would be impossible to hide. I could keep my back to him, but that wouldn't work for long.

My heart started to race when I realized this was the moment. Hades would know the truth, and it would change everything...for better or worse.

Probably for worse.

He came up behind me and placed his hands on my hips. A moment later, his chest pressed into my back, and he rested his chin on my head.

I was so still.

His deep voice was audible over the shower. "Can I join you?"

I could feel his arousal against my back, feel the way his fingers dug into my skin. I could tell he wanted me, that he was growing tired of waiting. He gave me subtle openings to see if I was ready to change my mind, but if I didn't take it, he let it go. "Yes."

His arms wrapped around my chest and over my arms, and he held me close, his arms a protective cage that kept all the bad thoughts out. We hadn't spoken much since he'd confronted me in my office a few days ago, and now he seemed apologetic about his behavior.

He bent his neck down and kissed me on the shoulder. Then his hands started to guide me in a circle, to turn me around so he could see my face.

I couldn't control my breathing. It went haywire, deep and fast. My heart was beating at a frenzied rate. If I weren't covered in water, I'd be sweating. When I made the full rotation, I looked him in the eye with fear written all over my face.

His eyes moved to mine, and he watched me for several seconds, taking in my features and reading them like words on a page. His hands went to my hips, and he probably thought my unease was because of this level of intimacy. "It's okay. It's me."

There was no going back, so I grabbed both of his hands and placed them over my stomach.

Instantly, he noticed the expanded curves of my body. His fingers lightly pressed into me in reaction. His chin dropped, and his eyes moved to my swollen belly. He didn't blink. He didn't move. He needed at least five seconds to process what I had just revealed to him. His reaction was blank, and now he was impossible to read.

He gently pulled his hands apart so he could see my full stomach. When he truly understood what he was looking at, he lifted his gaze and looked me in the eye. It took a moment for his surprise to fade away, for him to understand exactly what this meant. He'd walked into the bathroom thinking he could bring us closer together. Discovering I was pregnant was the very last thing he'd anticipated.

I waited for the questions, waited for the fear and anger.

Instead, his eyes softened like wilted flowers. He became so tender, his face taking on a boyish charm. His shoulders relaxed, and a gentle smile spread onto his lips. When his hand understood what his brain had absorbed, he gently rubbed it over my stomach, trying to connect to the life inside me.

It wasn't the reaction I'd expected. Instead of being relieved by it, I assumed he didn't understand the situation, that there was a possibility it wasn't his. That thought didn't seem to go through his head, so I needed to bring him back to reality. "I'm almost four months along."

His arm wrapped around my waist, and he pulled me closer as his other hand spanned my stomach.

I couldn't bring myself to say it, to admit that this might not be a happy moment between a husband and wife. "I'm not sure…"

He gave me a strong stare. "It's mine."

I wanted that to be true more than anything else. "But…"

"It's mine."

"We could always check."

He shook his head. "It doesn't matter what that says. I'll love this baby the same regardless."

I couldn't keep the surprise off my face. "Why?" He didn't seem like the kind of man that would want to do something like this, take on the burden of raising a child that may not even be his. He could be cold and ruthless, so it seemed like aborting it would be his initial response.

"Because half of it is you."

My heart started to slow once again, and my entire body relaxed. It was the first time I'd found peace in months, finally let the stress leave my shoulders.

"We can do the test, and if it says what we don't want to hear, I'll stand by whatever decision you make. But if this is something you wanna do, I'm here. I want whatever you want." He slid his hand into my hair and pulled our faces together. "But I know he's mine. I know that's my son. And I know I'm gonna love him so much it kills me."

I felt a small explosion inside my chest, adoration for this man. I never expected him to react this way, to be so supportive and loyal. Most men wouldn't feel this way, be my rock through all this heartache. My heart throbbed in a whole new way, and I suddenly felt lighter than air. I was the luckiest woman in the world to have him, and I owed my mother my gratitude for making me marry him in the first place. I never would've found joy with anyone else, wouldn't have the foundation and trust with anyone else. "Why do you assume it's a boy?"

He rested his forehead against mine. "I just know."

"And why do you assume it's yours?"

He closed his eyes as he held me. "Because I know."

HADES

I sat at a table in the middle of the bar, Ash and Damien with me. The bartender had left a bottle of scotch so we could drink as much as we wanted. The place was closed to the public, so it was just the three of us.

Ash spoke to Damien. "If we get rid of the dealers on the east side, all we have to worry about is the west and the ports. Maddox must understand what's going on by now. He could retaliate at any moment." He switched his gaze to me and opened his mouth like he was going to continue his line of thinking. But he shut his mouth again and narrowed his eyes. "What the fuck are you smiling about?"

I dragged my hand across my jawline, not even noticing.

Damien stared at me, his expression stoic. He didn't talk to me directly, only participated in the debate and left our personal relationship out of the mix.

Ash spoke again. "You really shouldn't mix alcohol with meth."

I set down my glass and told him the truth. "Sofia is pregnant."

Ash was in shock. "What? Are you serious? Since when?"

Damien didn't ask any questions. He didn't seem the least bit surprised. Instead of offering his congratulations, he grabbed his glass and took a drink.

"She's almost four months along. Now I understand why she's been so weird. Every time I made progress with her, we'd somehow go backward." She'd been keeping the secret from me for a long time. She probably was terrified of my reaction, terrified she was carrying the baby of the asshole who'd tortured her.

Ash did the math in his head. "Wait…doesn't that mean?"

I wouldn't entertain the idea. "It's mine."

"You got tested?" my brother asked.

"No." I shook my head. "I don't need to."

Ash looked at Damien as if he were hoping he would chime in. When Damien was quiet, Ash turned back to me. "I know it's not my place, but you should find out for sure. It could change everything."

I couldn't explain to him my sense of faith, the almost godlike experience I'd had with the gypsy in the bazaar. She'd read my future and told me I would have two sons, so I knew that baby was mine. "I don't need a test."

"Not to piss you off, but what if you're wrong?" Ash grew

more involved in the conversation because he was looking out for my best interests. "Do you really wanna raise a kid whose father did that to your wife? Does either one of you really want to do that?"

I didn't want to think about the possibility, but I knew how Sofia felt about it without even asking her. If abortion were an option, she would've confronted me sooner, asked for a test, and then aborted it if it was Maddox's. The fact that she didn't do that told me she wanted this baby no matter what. That was fine with me. It was half her, so of course I would love it. "Even if it's not mine, I'll still love it like it is. But that doesn't matter because I know it's mine."

"How can you be so sure?" Ash continued to press the topic.

"The gypsy told me I would have two sons with Sofia," I said. "And the timing makes it possible."

Damien was still quiet from his seat at the table.

Ash stared at me like it was just the two of us. "You can't trust gypsies. She said you would have two sons with Sofia. She never said Sofia wouldn't have children with somebody else. This is your fortune, not hers."

The thought made my fingertips cold, but it didn't change my faith. Sofia was my soul mate, so I knew we would work it out in spite of everything. If she were someone else, my reaction would be very different. If I were married to someone else, I probably would ask for an abortion if it wasn't mine. But with Sofia, it was totally different. "I accept whatever happens. If she wants to keep this baby, then I will be the father. Period."

Damien held his glass as he stared down at the contents. He'd mentally removed himself from the conversation. He used to be the guy in whom I confided all my secrets, but now my brother had taken his place.

"And not to be insensitive…" Ash wasn't going to let this go. "She should get tested, make sure everything is okay, you know?"

I nodded. "She already did that."

"And Maddox is a psychopath. His kid would probably be demon spawn." He leaned back in his chair and crossed his arms over his chest. "I couldn't do it."

"You could if you were in love." We were gathered there to discuss our plans for Maddox, but the conversation had turned into gossip hour. When I'd realized Sofia was pregnant, I knew I was happy. I didn't think about anyone else besides the two of us. It was a moment between lovers, a beautiful moment that changed our lives forever. In my heart, I believed she was having my first son and we were beginning a long life together. I'd given up on the idea of her loving me, and now I realized I didn't need it. She would love our son as much as I did, and since her son would be half of me, she would love me…in an indirect way.

That was good enough for me.

When I got home, it was late.

I shed my heavy coat and then stripped off everything else. My watch was slipped off my wrist and returned to my collection in the drawer. When I approached the bed, I realized she was awake.

In one of my white t-shirts with the sheets pulled to her shoulders, she looked so comfortable, but also wide awake.

I volunteered my whereabouts. "I was with Damien and Ash." I got into bed and lay beside her.

"I assumed."

I was glad she hadn't assumed I was doing something else. I came close to her and slid my hand underneath her shirt. My large hand covered her entire stomach, and I felt the little bulge that was full of life. When I saw her in the shower, it was the first time I'd seen her naked in months. It was a beautiful sight, but instead of focusing on her tits and curves, my eyes were focused on the way her stomach was slightly swollen. In that moment, that was all I cared about.

And she'd never looked sexier.

I wanted her more than I ever had before. Knowing she was pregnant with my son was such a carnal turn-on. My arousal was biological, evolutionary. It must be something all men felt when their woman was growing a child. The differences in her body were subtle, probably unnoticeable if you saw her every single day. But since I hadn't seen her beautiful skin in so long, I noticed the changes immediately. Her tits were a little bigger, her hips a little wider. There was more mass around her thighs and ass. Her body was changing in preparation for motherhood. And it was so damn hot.

She didn't flinch at my touch or seem uncomfortable with my desire. I couldn't pretend I wasn't deeply attracted to her. My dick had a mind of its own, and I couldn't quiet it if I tried, couldn't stop looking at her like I wanted her. She couldn't hold that against me.

"You are so beautiful." I pulled up her shirt slightly and pressed a kiss to her stomach. I wanted to kiss her everywhere, appreciate her body with my tongue, but I would keep my hormones in check until she verbally told me she was ready.

But if she made me wait any longer, I might explode.

Her fingers moved into my hair. "You think so?"

I angled my face back to hers. "Yes." I lay beside her, my head on the same pillow, and I rubbed my palm over her stomach. "I've never wanted you more." I didn't mean to make her uncomfortable, but that was the honest truth. I was a man deeply in love with my wife, and I wanted to make love to her all night until the sun rose the next morning.

Her eyes softened as she looked at me. "I was so scared to tell you."

"Never be scared to tell me anything."

Her eyes tilted down to my chest, and her fingers lightly stroked the muscles. "I thought you were going to leave."

She really had no idea I was in love with her. I'd sacrificed my body for her freedom. She thought I would do that for just anyone? She cared more about seeing the bad things in relationships; she was oblivious to the good. She waited for me to sneak off with another woman. So that was what she looked for. But since she never expected me to love her, she couldn't see it. "I'll never leave you, baby. We'll spend our lives together, die together, and then be buried together."

Her eyes softened again. "I don't know what I did to deserve you."

I had no idea why the universe thought I was worthy of her.

"Are you sure you don't want to find out if you're the father?" Her voice came out as a whisper. "I understand if you want to know."

"It really doesn't matter to me. It's up to you. But if we're gonna keep this baby regardless, then I don't see why it matters. If it weren't mine, would you want to abort it?"

She placed her hand over mine. "If that really happened...I don't think I could do it. I hate that man all the way down to my soul, but now that I can feel the life inside me, I just couldn't do it."

"Then we don't need to do a test. This is our baby. End of story."

It was the first time she'd smiled at me in months. Her hand squeezed the two of mine, and she released a deep sigh. "I was so scared. I was scared to lose you. I was scared to do this alone. It made me realize how much I need you. You are such a big part of my life now. You're my best friend, you're my husband, you're everything. When we got married, I didn't know how things were going to be, but I certainly didn't expect this. I didn't expect us to be so close. I didn't expect us to trust each other like this. And I didn't expect you to be such a good man to me." She couldn't meet my gaze, as if it was too hard. "After everything that happened, you were still there for me. I'm sorry I was difficult in the beginning of our marriage. I'm sorry I hurt you in the past. I'm so glad I married you, and I couldn't picture my life with anyone else."

I watched her stare down at our hands, and I was relieved I didn't have to hide my expression. Her words touched me down to my bones. She'd never said anything like that to me before, and it was such a relief to hear the emotion in her voice. I wasn't on the verge of tears, but I knew I was staring at her like she was the love of my life.

Because she was.

My hand cupped her cheek and slid into her hair as I moved toward her. I tugged her closer to me, making our bodies become one. Then my lips found hers, and I kissed her gently, slowly, with restrained passion. I couldn't make love to my wife with my body, but I could make love to her with her mouth, with my lips. I wanted to tell her that I loved her, just put the truth out there and deal with the consequences later. Even if she got angry, I didn't care. Even if she would never love me back. I still wouldn't regret saying it. I was a man who loved a woman.

And I wanted her to know that.

I felt like a new man.

There had been a stark separation between us for so long, and now that the barrier was removed, we felt like partners again, like husband and wife again. Now that her fears had been erased, she knew I was here for the long haul. She trusted me more now than she ever had before, and it even seemed like she felt something for me. Maybe she wasn't in love with me, but it seemed like she loved me.

Now she didn't hide in the bathroom to change. She was comfortable enough to step into the bedroom after her shower and look through her clothes until she found something she wanted to wear. Most of the time, she was completely naked, and after she slipped on her panties, she was a wet dream.

It was impossible not to stare.

The little bulge of her stomach was hardly noticeable. Until she put my hands on her tummy, I probably wouldn't have figured out the truth. But now that I knew there was life growing inside her, it was impossible not to notice.

I'd fallen in love with my wife for many reasons, reasons I couldn't even understand. I'd always admired her ambition, her cold sassiness, and the way she was so fiercely independent. But I'd be lying if I said her beauty didn't cast a spell over me.

I watched her stand in front of her closet and look for something to wear, her slightly damp hair cascading around her shoulders. She pushed the hangers to the left as she selected an outfit to wear to work, completely oblivious to my lust.

Her long legs were toned and beautiful. With slightly tanned skin and a fair complexion, she had a Tuscan hint to her features. She had a deep curve in her lower back that made her plump ass hypnotizing. With perfect posture, she carried herself like an invisible crown had been placed on her head. She contained royal elegance, a presence so captivating, she was addictive to the eyes.

Her face was her most gorgeous feature, with full lips, big eyes, and contoured cheekbones. Compared to all the beautiful women in the world, she might not stand out, but to me, she was the sexiest woman on the planet.

And she was mine.

I was sitting at the table watching her, ignoring my laptop in front of me. I was showered and ready to get dressed, but I continued to sit in my sweatpants and stare at her. She hadn't told she was ready, but she didn't refrain from parading her naked body in front of me.

Maybe it was time.

I wanted her so much, I was willing to try. Maybe after a

few kisses, she would reciprocate my desire. I could get her to stop thinking about the past and think about the present. I could get her to think about me and only me.

Plus, my dick was so hard I thought it might explode.

I shut my laptop and got to my feet. My hands slid into the pockets of my sweatpants, and I approached her from behind. My heart quickened in my chest, as if I actually felt nervous for the first time in my life. It was mostly excitement because I wanted this woman more than anything in the world. I stopped behind her, close enough to smell her shampoo, her perfume, the floral scent of the lotion she rubbed across her skin. She seemed oblivious to my presence, more focused on the black dress she was considering for the day.

My hands snaked around her waist and rested right over her belly. I pulled her toward me gently as I bent my neck down and placed a kiss on her exposed shoulder. The touch was innocent, the affection borderline tame. But when my lips felt her warm skin, there was a distinct shiver down my spine. I inhaled a deep breath through my nose and felt my fingers tighten their grip on her stomach. There was more excitement in the delicate embrace than I'd ever had with another woman. That simple kiss was the greatest foreplay I'd ever experienced.

She tightened noticeably under my touch, but she didn't push me away. Her fingers released the dress she was holding, but she didn't turn around.

My lips gave her another kiss on the neck, my mouth

opening so I could taste her skin on my tongue. I pulled her a little closer so she could feel my hard chest against her back. I wanted her to feel me…all of me. I wanted her to understand how much I wanted her, how much I desired her.

My kisses continued until I began to devour her. My mouth moved closer to her ear, wanting her to hear the way she made me pant with desire. I could grab her tit and squeeze it, but I preferred the little bump of her belly. It was her sexiest feature. I knew some men had a fetish for pregnant women, but I certainly had never been one of them.

That wasn't the case anymore.

She'd never been so sexy. I knew I didn't feel this way about all pregnant women. It was because she was my wife. And I knew the baby was mine. The longer I kissed her, the more excited I became. I was oozing in my boxers, and my muscles were tightening. It'd been so long since I'd had her, going on months now. I was a man with needs, and she was the only woman who could fulfill them.

I guided her around to face me so I could kiss those lips with the same passion that I kissed her everywhere else. My hand cupped her cheek, and I kissed her aggressively. I lost control and fell into the chemistry between our bodies. My hand pushed down the front of my boxers so I could get naked and take her to bed.

But then she extinguished the fire.

She pulled her face away and pressed her hands against my

chest to put distance between us. Her eyes fell as if she couldn't look me in the eye. "I'm not ready…"

Disappointment washed over me, and my body was so hot that even an ice bath couldn't cool me down. I would respect any request she made, never push her to do something she didn't want to do, but I thought she needed a nudge. "Baby, I'm not him."

"I know…"

"I'll wait as long as you want me to wait. But it's always going to be hard until we take that next step. We need to push through it and move on with our lives." I searched her face, hoping she would change her mind. I knew she wanted me, knew she still desired me. "It's you and me. It's different with us."

She wouldn't budge. "I'm sorry."

I swallowed all my frustration and let it disappear. This was something that couldn't be rushed, and I had to be patient a while longer. Once I composed myself, I slid my fingers under her chin and forced her gaze to rise to meet mine. "You are worth the wait." My arms circled her waist and brought her closer to my chest. My lips rested against her forehead, and I gave her a kiss. I was getting less action as a married man than I did as a bachelor, but that was okay. As long as we were still together, we would be okay.

SOFIA

I SAT ACROSS FROM HADES IN THE DINING ROOM DOWNSTAIRS. My mother sat beside me, rambling on about bullshit neither one of us cared about. I loved my mother, but since she'd lost her husband, she talked a million miles a minute because she didn't have anyone else to talk to. Sometimes, it was overwhelming for the two of us, especially Hades since he was a quiet man.

Hades drank from his wineglass and kept eating, his gaze averted and his mind somewhere else. Our relationship was slightly tense after the way I'd rejected him a few days ago. He didn't seem angry with me or resentful, but there was a hint of disappointment.

My mother continued to talk about the baby. "I hope it's a boy. I only have experience raising one daughter, so it'll be nice to do something different."

Hades seemed confident the baby was his, but sometimes I feared otherwise. It haunted me in the middle of the night when I couldn't sleep. The last thing I wanted was to give birth to my son or daughter and then see Maddox when I looked into their face. I wanted to be prepared.

When dinner was finished, my mother wouldn't stop talking, so I had to cut her off so we could go to bed. She didn't seem aware of Hades's annoyance, so she never took our subtle cues to be quieter. We said goodnight, and Hades and I walked up the stairs to our bedroom.

He was silent and a bit moody because he hated our family dinners. He wasn't so bitter about it when we tapered down our meals with my mother from five days a week to two. But now, it seemed like even two days were too much.

Instead of pointing it out, I chose to be more positive. "Thank you for putting up with her."

He continued to face forward as he walked beside me.

"I know she talks a lot. She's just lonely."

He cleared his throat before he spoke. "It's fine."

I knew it wasn't fine, but I appreciated him saying that anyway. I grabbed his hand and held it.

He squeezed mine in response.

When we entered the bedroom, we got ready for bed. I continued to undress in front of him and didn't shield my body from his gaze. He didn't look at me or make me uncomfortable. He took my request seriously and backed off. In fact, he purposefully turned his head away whenever

I was unclothed, as if the sight of me was too much to handle.

He sat up in bed, shirtless against the headboard. He held his phone between his fingers, and he seemed to be reading emails and paperwork.

I got under the sheets on my side of the bed and turned to him.

When he felt my stare, he set his phone on the nightstand and gave me his full attention. He turned off the bedside lamp and then cuddled up to me. He pulled our bodies close together, and as always, he was hard in his boxers. He immediately closed his eyes like he was ready to go to sleep.

"Hades?"

He opened his eyes again.

"I want to know."

His eyes narrowed slightly.

"I want to know if you're the father."

His expression didn't change. His eyes didn't convey annoyance or relief. He was a closed book, his thoughts a mystery. He'd been quieter lately after our incident in the closet, more withdrawn, like he needed his own space at the moment. "Okay."

"What does that mean?" I couldn't tell if he approved of my request or was indifferent to it.

His eyes remained locked on mine. "I'll do whatever you want."

"But it doesn't bother you?"

He shrugged. "Whatever those results are, they don't make a difference. But if you need to know, then I understand." He was far more supportive of this than I ever could've imagined.

I wasn't sure I would handle it so well if I were in his place. "I wish I could be calm like you."

"It's different for me than it is for you. And I already know what the results are going to say."

I gently rubbed my fingers against his chest. "How can you be so sure?"

"I just know the universe wouldn't let that happen to us."

"You mean God?" We never talked about our religious beliefs. We both came from Italian families, so it was just assumed we were both Catholic. But based on his career choice, perhaps I was wrong.

"Maybe. I know someone is looking out for me. I just don't know who."

"So you think everything that happens to us is fate?"

He considered the question carefully. "No. But I think someone will always give you a new path...if you need one." His hand moved to my stomach, and he gently stroked his fingers over the surface. "We'll see the doctor tomorrow. You'll get your answer then."

"I wish I could be as confident as you."

"Don't compare yourself to me. We've experienced vastly different things."

But I still wished I had the same kind of faith. I'd lost my faith a long time ago, long before Maddox took me. I didn't trust relationships or men. But all of that changed once I gave Hades a real chance. He was everything he claimed to be. "I also want to know if it's a boy or a girl."

"Do you have a preference?"

"No. I just want to know. You aren't the least bit curious?"

"I already know it's a boy."

I rolled my eyes. "There's no way you could possibly know that."

"Then I guess we'll see…"

"Does that mean you never want to have a girl?"

"I never cared either way." His expression slowly fell. "But now I feel a little differently about it."

I dropped my gaze, knowing exactly what he meant by that.

He was quiet for a while, his thoughts drifting away to a different place. He eventually closed his eyes, and his fingers stopped moving against my stomach. I knew he wasn't drifting off to sleep because his breathing hadn't changed.

But he needed the silence anyway to cleanse his thoughts of the disturbing images in his head.

"Don't feel bad for me. Don't think that way. I'm here with you now…and I'm happy."

———

We sat side by side in the doctor's office. My legs were crossed, and I was shaking my ankle because I was so nervous. The white room felt sterile, and that blankness made me more agitated. The results I was about to receive would change my life. A part of me didn't want to know. But the other part knew not knowing would haunt me.

Hades was in his dark suit because he had been at the bank prior to our doctor's appointment. One ankle rested on the opposite knee, and he looked so relaxed, like he was about to go into a massage or something. He adjusted his watch and glanced at the time before he turned his gaze to my shaking ankle. His large hand reached out and grabbed my thigh, and he steadied it with a strong grasp. He gave it a gentle squeeze before a whisper escaped his lips. "Baby."

I stilled at his words.

"It'll be alright."

I took a deep breath and slowly released it from my lungs. I closed my eyes and tried to think of a beautiful meadow.

"I am the father. I promise you."

I turned to look at him, needing the assurance in his gaze.

He moved his hand to mine and squeezed it. "And even if it's not, it doesn't change anything. It doesn't change this." He brought my hand to his lips and placed a soft kiss on my knuckles. The stubble on his jawline lightly brushed against my skin, scratching it.

The doctor walked inside a moment later, and he looked through the papers in our file. First, he told us the gender of our baby. "Congratulations. You're having a boy."

My hands squeezed his a little harder as I saw a glimpse of my future. I imagined a little boy running around the house, giggling without me far behind him. He had brown eyes and dark hair, a handsome boy who would become a handsome man like his father. But then the dread hit my heart again when I realized I had no idea who the father even was.

Hades kept his eyes on me even though the doctor was talking. "I told you we were having a son."

"Yeah, I just hope you're right about the other thing too."

The doctor pulled out a paper from the file and placed it on the counter beside us. "The paternity test checks out. Mr. Lombardi, you are a match."

Hades didn't react at all, not even a blink. A smile didn't creep onto his lips because he wasn't happy at the news. How could he be happy when he'd already known he was going to be the father?

I grabbed the paper off the counter and looked at it with my own eyes. "Oh my god..."

"I told you."

The doctor excused himself from the room, and we were left alone.

My hands started to shake as I held the results. Without my even realizing it, tears welled in my eyes. The drops became so big, they fell and splattered on the page. My chest ached with both pain and relief. I'd been terrified to raise the child of my tormentor. I would've loved that child anyway, but I would love it so much more if Hades was the father. Hundreds of pounds of weight were lifted from my shoulders. And I could finally breathe again. That asshole had no hold over me anymore. I never had to think about him again. I could move on with my life without looking back.

Hades wrapped his arm around my shoulders and pulled me close. He held me as I sobbed and made the ink run on the paper. My makeup was destroyed, and my mascara trailed like rivers down my cheeks. This was what I'd wanted more than anything else...to have this baby with my husband.

"It's alright, baby." His hand moved to my stomach, and he cupped it with his large palm. "We're a family...the three of us."

I could barely speak through my tears. "I was so scared. I wanted you to be the father. I needed you to be the father. I'm so happy it's you. You've been such a good husband to me, and I know you'll be an incredible parent."

His eyes stilled as he looked into mine, caught off guard by what I said. It seemed like he wanted to disagree with what I'd just said, but he never did. "I'll spend my life taking care of both of you. The two of you are the most important things in the world to me."

I looked into his eyes and saw sincerity shine through. "I know."

I was a whole different person.

I was living in a dream, the kind you never wanted to wake up from. My life was stable once again, and I was actually happy. Now that I knew Hades was the father of my son, I was so excited to be a mother. I was excited to start our family. I didn't know how I was going to balance my job and my kids, but I was determined to figure it out. I could leave the kids with my mother, but I didn't want her to watch them. I wanted to watch them.

I sat in the office at the hotel, my thoughts drifting to baby clothes and diapers, when my phone rang. It was Damien, so I answered. "I have some really good news…"

His tone was always melancholy now. With Hades still so cold to him, Damien seemed to have lost his spirit. It was profound in his tone of voice, the way he always seemed half asleep or depressed. "Yeah?"

"Just got the results from the doctor and Hades is the father." It was ironic that I talked to Damien as a friend when Hades wasn't even his friend anymore. I was used to having Damien in our lives, and it felt odd that he wasn't there anymore. He'd screwed up big time, but I knew his heart was in the right place. He cared about me, and he certainly cared about Hades.

"That's fucking great. Thank God."

"Yeah, I was pretty scared. Hades was so confident that the baby was his, so he didn't seem concerned about it. But I was a total wreck."

"Yeah, Hades has a sixth sense when it comes to stuff like that."

He was passionate about his decisions and so stubborn that he could never change his mind. He thought he was right about everything...and maybe he was. "I'm so happy he was right."

"Good. Now you can move on. And congratulations on the baby. I don't think I ever told you that."

I leaned back in my chair and crossed my legs under my desk. "Thank you. We weren't ready to start a family just yet, but I'm glad that it happened."

"Hades will be a good father. He's the best guy I know."

Listening to the pain in his voice made me so sad. "He'll come around."

He sighed loudly, like he didn't agree with that statement at all. "It's his birthday on Thursday. That's why I'm calling, just so you know. He's not big on celebrating his birthday, so I know he would never tell you."

He was right. It never came up, and I never asked. "Thanks for the heads-up."

"My best advice is don't make it a big deal. He doesn't like a lot of attention."

"Why is that?"

"I don't know. Probably because his family is dead and his brother hates him. Well, he used to hate him."

My hand moved to my stomach. "Well, he has a family now."

21

HADES

IT WAS LOUD IN THE CLUB. BASS FROM THE MUSIC VIBRATED from the speakers, and nearly naked ladies passed around glasses of booze.

Damien and I sat in our private booth, leather seats with a black table. We had glasses of scotch, but various drinks were piling up from admirers. Damien accepted the glasses with a wink in their direction. But I just ignored mine.

It was the perfect place for our conversation, because nobody could eavesdrop. It was so fucking loud. Damien kept several feet between us, treating me like he was the one who was pissed. He didn't try to rectify our relationship. He seemed to have let it go. "Maddox is hurting. We've sabotaged most of his distributors, and his drugs are disappearing from the streets. It's only a matter of time before that fucker shows his face."

"And I wonder how he'll do that."

Damien grabbed an extra drink sitting at the end of the

table. "With a normal person, I'd say he'd threaten us. But with this psychopath, he'll probably throw you a parade or some shit. Fucking weirdo. I would assume he's gay for you except for the fact..." He looked away, clearly embarrassed by what he'd just said. "Never mind."

He'd shoved his foot in his mouth, but I let it go. "You're probably right. He'll call me."

"I've been trying to track him down, and I think he's in the city."

"What makes you think that?"

"It's what the guys on the streets are telling me. But you never know, that information could be bullshit. With other guys, they're pretty straightforward. But Maddox reminds me of a fucking clown. He's always putting on a show. You never know what's real and what's not."

I couldn't wait until he was dead.

Damien watched a pretty girl walk by before he turned his gaze back to me. "I heard the good news."

I raised an eyebrow. "What good news?"

Two women approached our table. Both brunettes and both familiar. The first one on the left addressed us. "Hey, Hades." She gave me a flirtatious wave. Her eyes shifted back to Damien. "Hey."

It took me a second to recognize them. We'd been on a double date before. Or a double fuck...that was more accurate. They were both nice girls, so I was nice back. "How are things?"

"Good." The first brunette turned her eyes back on me. "A little cold for my liking, but I'll survive. You two look like you're having a heated conversation. We'll swing by later." She winked and walked away with her friend.

I forgot about them the second they were gone. "What good news?"

Damien's eyes watched them for a long time, his mind in the gutter and far away from this conversation. When they disappeared into the bathroom, he finally paid attention to me. "That the kid belongs to you."

I raised an eyebrow. "How did you know that?"

Damien rested his fingers on his glass as he considered a response. "Ash told me."

I'd mentioned it in passing to him the other day. Since they worked together, that was plausible.

"Well, I'm happy for you."

I gave a slight nod in acknowledgment. I wanted to say more, but I was still so livid with him. When hatred grew to indifference, that meant the relationship was beyond saving. Right now, I just hated him...and I couldn't stop. I blamed him for everything.

"You'll be a good father."

"Are we done here?" I didn't want to have these kinds of

conversations anymore. It was a conversation between friends, not adversaries.

Damien couldn't stop the hurt from entering his face. "Only business, huh?"

"Yes. Business only."

Damien looked like he was going to slam the glass down and shatter it. Rage filled his eyes, and he writhed in silence. Then he stood up abruptly, prepared to depart. "I'm done apologizing to you. I'm sorry about what happened. But you need to take responsibility for what happened too. If you really wanted to settle down and have a quiet life, you should've left. But you didn't. Don't put that shit on me."

I should have gone home, but Damien's final words continued to echo in my mind. The loud music muffled my thoughts but didn't silence them altogether. My hand was wrapped around the glass, and I stared at the contents, unsure what drink I was on. Alone, I sat in the bar like I had no one to go home to.

When he'd walked off, I'd almost chased after him and broke his jaw. But I reminded myself he wasn't worth my time, so I just let him go. Was there any merit to what he said? Had he been right? Was I the one to blame for what happened to my wife?

I couldn't carry that guilt.

I already carried all of her pain and sadness. And with every nightmare she had, I felt that agony more and more. Once we confirmed that the baby was mine, she seemed to relax a bit, but the fact that she wouldn't sleep with me told me that she wasn't okay.

Maybe she would never be okay.

"You look miserable." The brunette I'd seen earlier slid into the booth beside me. She had a cosmo with her, and her deep blue dress was short and very revealing for January. She gave me a gentle nudge in the arm. "You're too hot to be miserable."

We'd slept together sometime in the past, but I couldn't quite remember when. It was some time after Sofia dumped me, and I was in so much pain. I fucked everyone to forget her, but there weren't enough beautiful women in the world to accomplish that. I wasn't in the mood to talk, just brood in silence, so I said nothing.

"Did you and Damien get into a fight?" She continued to sit beside me, far too close considering all the vacant seats around us.

"No. We just aren't friends anymore."

Her eyes filled with sadness. "That's too bad. You guys are cute together."

"Don't say shit like that."

She brushed off my insult. She looked at her glass for a

while and tapped her long nails against the surface. "You want to get out of here?"

My hand grabbed my glass, so maybe she didn't see my wedding ring. I placed my palm on the surface so it was unmistakable. "I'm married."

She didn't look at my hand. "I know."

I pulled my hand away, slightly offended that my status didn't matter to her. Cheating never used to bother me. I'd bedded married women before, guilt-free. My sense of morality was nonexistent. But all of that changed when I met Sofia. "I'm not that kind of guy."

"Really? Then why are you sitting alone in a bar? Happily married men don't go to bars. The ones who do are always unhappy, and they are always looking for something to make themselves feel better. You fit that description perfectly."

Yes, I was miserable. I'd lost my best friend, and my wife was still disturbed by what had happened to her. I didn't know how to kill my enemy, and I hadn't had sex in so long, I was starting to lose my mind. Without it, I felt lost. All the frustrations that bubbled under the skin couldn't escape. My wife's rejection wounded me, and I pretended it wasn't a big deal so I wouldn't look like an ass, but I was really disappointed. One of the things I loved most in my relationship with Sofia was gone.

She moved her hand to my thigh. "Come home with me."

I could feel her fingers dig into my thigh, feel her hand

migrate to where my dick was located. If I found release tonight, no one would ever know. It didn't mean anything to me, just a way to cure the loneliness. The fact that I let this moment happen at all told me how lost I was. This wasn't me. And if it was, I didn't want it to be. I grabbed her wrist and pushed it away. "I am gonna go home, but to my wife."

I never told Sofia what happened at the bar. A part of me felt like a liar and a cheater. I shouldn't have let that moment go as far as it did. But I also knew, at the end of the day, I said no. I didn't give in to the temptation and went home where I belonged.

I said no. That was what mattered.

So, I said nothing. It would make her feel insecure. It would make her feel guilty for not sleeping with me, and I didn't want to rush her into something she wasn't ready for. I wanted her to be with me because she wanted it, not because she was scared to lose me.

I walked into her office and saw her sitting at her desk. Her silky hair was pulled back, revealing her beautiful face and full lips. Her green eyes were down and reading reports. She was in a sweater dress and knee-high boots.

I stared at her for a second, feeling the guilt eat me alive. My wife was so beautiful. How could I think, even for a second, about someone else? She was pregnant with my son, and I loved her so much. I knew I'd only felt that way because it had been a rough couple of months. But I still felt so shitty.

When she realized I was in the room, she looked up and noticed me. A smile full of sunshine appeared on her lips as she looked so thrilled to see me standing there. "Wow, it's five already?" She gathered her papers and organized them in the drawers.

I inched farther into the room and watched her beautiful figure as she moved to clean up her desk. Constantly being reminded how sexy she was didn't help these desperate urges in my body.

When she finished, she came around the desk and embraced me. Her arms moved around my shoulders and she kissed me, her soft lips moving against mine for a kiss that was full of hot breaths and a little bit of tongue.

My hands glided over her body, feeling the deep curve in her back and the little bulge in her stomach. My hands wanted to grab her ass and squeeze, but I stayed away from particular areas. This kiss was enough to get me hot and bothered, to think about throwing her on the desk and taking her how I wanted. I couldn't be myself, couldn't be the man I really was. I was forced to be patient, respectful, and celibate.

I couldn't do this for any other woman.

She pulled away but kept her face close to mine. "You want to go out to dinner tonight?"

We never went anywhere. After what happened, Sofia had

wanted to stay home. This was a curve ball, but after what she'd been through, I would do whatever she wanted. "Sure."

"What's your favorite place?"

"We don't have to go where I wanna go. Where do you wanna go?"

"I think you have good taste, so I trust you." She leaned in and gave me another kiss on the mouth. This time, it was quick and gentle. When she looked me in the eye, there was a bright look of affection, like the way she used to look at me.

Maybe I just needed to wait a little longer. "Then let's go."

***

She sat across from me at the dinner table, wearing a backless cocktail dress. Her wedding ring reflected the flickering lights from the candles, and a diamond bracelet was on her other wrist. Her long hair was down and around her shoulders, and the lighting in the restaurant made her look so beautiful, she seemed fake. She held the menu open with her hands, her chin tilted down as her eyes shifted back and forth to read the entrees.

Fuck, I'd better get laid tonight.

This was fucking torture. She got all dressed up like a goddamn model, and that backless dress showed the sexy curves that distracted me. It was like she was trying to seduce me, trying to remind me what I was missing. If this was all just a tease, I'd probably lose my shit and blow up on her. I had to keep reminding myself what she'd been through, and I'd be a terrible person if I wasn't understanding.

But damn, this woman was killing me.

Even the way she took a drink of her water was sexy. Her plump lips left red lipstick all over the glass, and I couldn't stop picturing that same smear around my mouth, down my neck, and all over the base of my dick.

With her eyes still on the menu, she asked, "What are you getting?"

I wished I could order pussy. "Sirloin."

"I'm thinking about getting the chicken. I'd rather have pasta, but all those carbs."

I glanced at her small body and almost rolled my eyes. She had no idea that she was a perfect ten. No idea that she had a perky ass, a tiny waist, and nice big titties? If she needed to be reminded, she needed to let me fuck her. She wouldn't forget how perfect she was.

When the waitress came over to take our order, I ordered for both of us. "I'll have the steak. Well done. My wife will have the spaghetti." I grabbed both of the menus and handed them over.

A slight smirk came onto her lips. "That was smooth."

"Order what you want."

"Now that I'm pregnant, it'll be easy to gain weight."

"Then gain weight. That's what you're supposed to do when you're eating for two."

Her smile grew. "That's a nice thing to say. You don't care if I get big and fat?"

She could walk around in a burlap sack, and I would be just as attracted to her. "Not at all."

She stared at me for a while before she grabbed a piece of bread. "How's work?"

I never liked to talk about work. "I haven't found him. But I will."

"I meant the bank."

I shrugged. "Nothing new."

"Nothing?"

"I've been working with some offshore companies in Panama. Some of my clients are from the US, and since they own shipping companies, they need to claim those assets elsewhere. I'm also laundering their money just to make sure everything is safe." My bank wasn't for regular people with regular jobs. My business solely ran on corruption. But that was the only way to make money...through corruption.

She listened to every word like she was actually interested in what I had to say. "How did you get into that line of work?"

"I dropped out of university and made friends with the right people. I hustled to get the experience I needed, and once I qualified for my first loan, I started my own bank. One thing led to another, and that business grew."

"I remember my father said you were a smart and accomplished young man."

I wasn't young anymore. My thirties were passing quicker than my twenties. "I wouldn't consider myself to be smart. Just ambitious."

"Well, I think you're smart. Actually, I know you're smart."

The smartest thing I ever did was marry her.

She and I talked about the Tuscan Rose and other things related to work, and I realized it was one of the first times we'd talked about normal things. It reminded me how passionate she was about the hotel and her family's legacy. I saw the ambitious and savvy woman I'd met years ago. It reminded me why I fell in love with her in the first place. In the meantime, our dinner was served, and we ate in comfortable silence.

I loved having dinner with her when it was just the two of us. Sofia didn't ramble on like most women. She was comfortable with the silence like I was. That was why I hated her mother. That bitch never shut up.

Sofia ate most of her food quickly, showing she was truly hungry. Her hormones probably kicked up her appetite, and she needed more calories to take care of two people instead of one. She clearly enjoyed her food, which was good because the last thing she needed to worry about was calories and carbs. "Have you thought about names?"

I stared at her blankly, not understanding the question.

"Baby names."

No, I hadn't given it any thought at all. I was very happy about my son, but my mind was in the gutter lately. All I really cared about right now was getting laid. Maybe my future son would think I was insensitive, but when he became a man, he would understand. "No."

"Well, I have."

"Let's hear it."

She set down her fork and abandoned her food for the moment. Now that she was talking about our child, she lit up like Christmas morning. "I really like it, so don't shoot it down right away."

I wasn't picky about names, but I did want my son to have a strong and masculine name. "Alright."

"Since this is our firstborn and we may not have another boy…"

No, we would have another boy.

"What if we name him Andrew?"

I stared at her for several seconds because I couldn't believe what she'd just said. The suggestion practically blindsided me. I hardly identified with that name anymore. I'd been

Hades for so long, my former identity was practically forgotten.

She studied my reaction.

When I found my words, I spoke. "Why would you want to name him that?"

"Why wouldn't I want to name my son after his father?"

Her admiration for me had never been so obvious. For years, it was impossible to get her to see me as more than just a fuck buddy. I gave her everything, but she was never impressed. But now, everything felt different. It seemed like this woman adored me, respected me. She clearly trusted me, relied on me for everything. She used to be so stubborn and independent, but now she actually leaned on me. I was so speechless, and I didn't know what to say. It made me feel like an asshole for being so frustrated by her distance in the bedroom. I'd actually let another woman touch me because I was so parched from this dry spell. I knew I was a man behaving like a man, but that was no excuse. I needed to get my shit together.

She continued to study my gaze. "Is that okay?"

I cleared my throat. "We can name him whatever you want."

"But I want you to love the name too."

I'd never considered being a namesake. I'd never considered myself worthy of such an honor. But I did like the idea of having a son who carried my name, who carried my legacy, who would be there for Sofia when I was gone. "Yes. I like it."

"Great." A beautiful smile came onto her lips. "That was easier than I thought it was going to be."

"Why?"

"Because you're so stubborn."

"I'm stubborn?" I asked incredulously. I pointed my finger into my chest because I couldn't believe she threw that accusation at me. "Come on, baby. You are the most stubborn person I've ever met."

"Am not." She grabbed her glass of water and took a drink.

I cocked an eyebrow and gave her an expression full of accusation. She was impossible to tie down because she was ornery like a wild horse. I'd asked her to marry me once, and she'd dumped me in response. When she came to live with me, she wanted her own room. I had to force everything to happen because nothing would've transpired if she had it her way.

She avoided my gaze for a few seconds. After pressing her lips together tightly, she finally looked at me again. "Okay... I'm a little stubborn."

I wanted to roll my eyes, but instead, an uncontrollable smile came onto my lips. Sometimes she aroused me, sometimes she impressed me, but during times like these, she made me fall just a little harder. She made me think she was cute, made me appreciate the fact that she was only mine. "Whatever you say, baby."

We returned home and entered the bedroom. Outside on the terrace, white candles were placed around the stone railing. In the center of the table was a tray of hot coffee along with sugar and cream. Helena had never done anything like this before, and I suspected she did it because she remembered it was my birthday.

Sofia didn't seem surprised as she walked outside into the freezing cold. She wore her thick coat over her backless dress, and she took a seat in one of the chairs. "You want some coffee?"

"I only drink coffee in the morning."

"Well, you're gonna be a father. Time to cut back on the scotch." She patted the table with her palm, calling me to her like I was a dog.

I obeyed because this woman turned me into a pussy-whipped little bitch. I sat in the chair across from her and took the cup she made for me. I took a drink and let the hot liquid warm my insides.

She held her cup between her hands, like she was using it to keep warm. The lining of her coat wrapped around her neck and protected her from the winter chill. She looked even more beautiful out here than she had in the restaurant. It seemed like she had that pregnant glow, but she wasn't far enough along to possess the quality. Maybe it was just in my head. Or maybe she always had a glow…to me.

I knew she was cold pretty much all the time. Even in the summer, her skin was cold to the touch in bed. She snuggled into my side and stole all my warmth. "If you're cold, we can go inside."

"I like it out here."

I drank my coffee as I continued to look at her, unable to believe we were in this moment. She used to hate me, but now she was my best friend. I couldn't divulge every secret that I kept, but she was still the closest person to me. We were partners, we were allies, and like gangsters, I would take a bullet in the chest for her.

"There's something I want to give you…"

Fuck.

She reached into her jacket pocket and pulled out a small box. It was wrapped in blue wrapping paper, images of balloons on the surface. There was a black bow on top. It was clearly a birthday present, and now I realized she'd planned this entire evening. It wasn't a spontaneous date night; it was a celebration. But she didn't mention that because she knew I didn't want the attention.

She pushed the box farther toward me. "Open it."

I was annoyed that she wanted to celebrate a day I didn't give a damn about. I wanted to interrogate her to know the person who'd given up my secret. But then I remembered it didn't matter. This was my wife—she deserved to know when my birthday was. And if she wanted to celebrate with me, pick something out for me, I should feel grateful. Truth be told, there was no one else I'd rather spend this day with.

I took the box and ripped off the paper. Inside was a slender black box. I pulled off the top and saw the silver watch inside. It was an Omega, one of the most expensive watches on the market. I knew she had money, but I didn't want her to spend it on me. But I was so touched by the thoughtful gift that I didn't dare complain.

I lifted it out of the box to get a better look. My eyes moved up to her face, and I saw the suppressed smile on her lips. There was also emotion in her eyes, like she was about to cry. I looked at the watch again and ran my thumb over the face. "I love it. Thank you."

"I thought you could add it to your collection."

There was no collection anymore. This was the only watch I would ever wear. I unclasped the watch on my right wrist and removed it. It was one from the collection in my drawer, something I'd picked out on my own. I was about to slip the new one on when she stopped me.

"It's engraved."

I paused before I turned over the watch to read the back. In a feminine script very like her own was the engraving in the metal.

I love you.

I stared at the three words but couldn't trust the information my eyes were relaying to my brain. It seemed like a dream, a trick my mind played on me. Instead of reading what I was supposed to read, I just pretended it said what I wanted to see. But I read it again.

I love you.

It must've been at least ten seconds of me staring. I'd loved this woman for so long, so many years, and I'd abandoned the notion that she could ever feel the same way. Just when I thought I'd broken the curse, the most terrible thing happened to her, and I thought I'd lost my chance forever.

But it looked like I was getting another shot.

It looked like I'd accomplished the impossible. I righted my wrongs, I atoned for my sins, and I became worthy of the woman I loved. I became the man she needed, became the man who was ready to accept his soulmate.

Instead of just feeling unbridled joy, I actually felt pain. It was too good to be true, made me wonder if this was a dream. I wanted this so much, and I couldn't believe it was happening. All those years of heartache had been worth it. Watching her leave me had been worth it. Everything I did to get here had been worth it.

My hand shook slightly as I held the watch, and I eventually gripped it tightly in my fist. I lifted my gaze to meet hers, to look her in the eye for the first time. But instead of meeting my gaze head on, her eyes were down on her coffee.

The woman who wasn't afraid of anything...was afraid

of me.

She was afraid of my rejection, afraid I wouldn't feel the same way. Now, she thought she might have sabotaged our relationship, that all the closeness we'd achieved had been destroyed.

How could she be so blind?

How could she not see how much I loved her?

I put the watch on my wrist and clasped it into place. "Look at me."

She took a deep, audible breath then raised her chin to look me in the eye. She was still scared, afraid of whatever I would say next. Like a prisoner waiting for their verdict from a judge, she could barely keep herself together.

I wanted to tell her the complete truth, that I was stupidly in love with her, that I'd been in love with her for years. I wanted to tell her that I married her because my heart wouldn't stop beating for her. I wanted to tell her that she was my soul mate. But that seemed like too much, too many words to describe what I felt. "I love you too."

The moment felt right.

Once I read those words from her heart, I became a new man. Somehow, I loved her more. I fell even deeper in love. After all the heartbreak we'd suffered, I finally felt like I was put back together. My scars and bruises were gone, and I somehow felt stronger than I had ever been before. Her love healed me, made me new.

I stood in front of her in our bedroom, the patio doors closed and the candles still flickering in the window. My eyes were locked on to hers as I moved in closer. I pushed my jacket over my shoulders and let it fall to the floor. It was so quiet I could hear it thud against the rug. My hands moved to her coat, and I slowly pushed it off, let it slide down her slender arms until she was in just her black dress. I could see the slight hesitation in her eyes, but I could also see the love I'd never noticed before.

My arms moved around her back, and I gently pulled her closer to me. My bare hands felt her soft skin, the small muscles that surrounded her spine. My fingertips could feel her frantic pulse under her skin. I brought our faces close together and held her like we were dancing. I wanted to kiss her but didn't want to start something she wasn't prepared to finish. In any other context, I wouldn't say a word to ruin this beautiful moment, but I couldn't be wrong about something like this. "May I make love to you?" All the lust was gone from my body because that was not what I wanted from her. I wanted her soul, her heart, and everything else in between.

She held my gaze without flinching, her hands slowly moving to my chest, where she fidgeted with the top button of my collared shirt. Her eyes slowly moved down to my lips like she wanted to kiss me, like she wanted to feel me as much as I wanted to feel her. A minute passed as we stood together in the darkness, the tension rising between us. Her hand suddenly tightened on my shirt as she tugged me to her.

Then she kissed me.

My lips were paralyzed by her touch because it felt like I was launched back in time. It felt the way it used to, like there was no one else except the two of us. Her soft lips moved with mine, taking control like she wasn't the least bit afraid. She breathed into my mouth before she gently sucked my bottom lip. Her fingers tightened on my shirt, tugging a little harder. Her small tongue moved into my mouth next, and she kissed me a little harder, a little deeper.

Overwhelmed by the electricity in my veins, I was frozen by her deep affection. It took me a few seconds to truly accept what was happening. My hands slid into her hair, and I pulled her closer to me, kissing her with deep, passionate embraces. I got lost in her right away, feeling reunited with the woman I loved.

My hand moved to the back of her neck, where the top of her dress was tied. My fingers gently tugged on the bow until it came loose. Once the knot was free, the dress slid down her body and fell to the floor at her feet. She stood in nothing other than a simple black thong, but that little piece of underwear was sexier than any piece of lingerie.

Her fingers unbuttoned my shirt as she kept kissing me, as our lips moved faster to enjoy each other. Our breaths deepened and grew louder as we quickened the pace. When my shirt was free, she pushed it over my shoulders so it could fall to the floor along with everything else.

With my hand still in her hair, I backed her up to the bed. I'd never wanted her more than I did now. It seemed like the last few years didn't even matter. Our lives together really started when she told me those three words. It was a new beginning, and this felt like our first time together. I could love her openly and deeply and knew it wouldn't drive her away. I could tell her how I really felt without intimidation. I could love her with my whole heart and knew she would feel the same way.

She yanked on my belt and got it loose before she dropped my zipper and got my slacks over my hips. She pushed on my boxers next, her lips still making love to mine. When my pants and my shoes were gone, I was naked and ready to take her. I'd never been so hard in my life, never wanted a woman more.

My hands pushed her panties over her hips and ass, and when they got to her thighs, they fell to her ankles on their own. I guided her onto the bed where her head could rest on a pillow. Our bodies were on top of the sheets, and she looked up at me with nothing but arousal in her eyes.

I held myself on top of her, positioning myself between her thighs. One of my large hands slid into her hair, and I looked into her gaze like I never wanted to stop. There was nowhere else I would rather be. Even if we were both broken, together, we were fixed. Just when I was about to ask her if she had any second thoughts, she spoke.

Her hands moved over my chest until her fingers slipped into my hair. She pulled me closer to her and locked her ankles around my waist. "Husband, make love to me."

22

SOFIA

I woke up next to Hades.

He was flat on his back with his hand resting on his tight stomach. His face was slightly tilted toward me, and he looked so peaceful when he was asleep. He wasn't the hard and dangerous man who hunted the streets of Florence. He was soft...kind.

A shadow of hair was sprinkled across his jaw, and his powerful chest rose and fell gently as he rested in his deep sleep. He looked like a new man to me—not just my husband, but the love of my life. He was everything to me, and I couldn't picture my life with anyone else.

I had no idea how I got here. I didn't want to marry this man until I was forced. Our marriage was poison in my veins, and I refused to let him under my skin. But one day, everything changed. My affectionate feelings somehow amplified and became powerful. My heart grew three times in size just so I could have the ability to love him. When

Maddox took me away, Hades did whatever he could to get me back...even sacrificed himself. It broke my heart to watch him take my place, but I also admired his unflinching loyalty to me. Not all men would do that.

Not all men would die for their wives.

I rested my cheek on his shoulder with my arm around his waist. I had to go to the hotel today, but I wanted to stay right there next to him. I lived in bliss, and I wasn't ready to let that feeling go.

When I told him I loved him, I really thought he wouldn't say it back.

Thankfully, he did.

I eventually got out of bed and got ready for the day. After I showered and styled my hair, I returned to the bedroom to pick out something from my closet.

He was awake, standing in his black sweatpants without a shirt. The curtains behind him were open, letting the winter sun stretch across the rug. With his thick arms resting by his sides, he looked at me...really looked at me. It was the kind of stare he used to give me all the time, years ago when we were clandestine lovers. It was a look full of possession, desire, and something much deeper. We hadn't exchanged a single word last night after we went to bed. The night was spent with our bodies moving together, carrying on a silent conversation that didn't need words.

But now that the sun was up, everything was different.

He slowly moved toward me, his bare feet audible against the floor. He was a heavy man, strong like a horse and thick like a bear. His presence was potent and overwhelming, like he could control me without lifting a finger. When he was directly in front of me, he tilted his chin down slightly to meet my look.

I was paralyzed by him in a way I had never been before. Butterflies fluttered in my tummy, and I could feel my quickened pulse in my neck. My chest rose a little higher to get more air into my lungs. My lips suddenly felt hot, as if I could feel his warm tongue against my mouth without even touching him. I saw Hades in a whole new way. He was the most desirable man in the world. He was strong and powerful, deadly sexy, and had the loyalty of a king.

And he was mine.

He stared at me for what felt like an eternity. His eyes shifted back and forth as they looked into mine, as if he were experiencing the same emotions that I was. He was comfortable in the silence, so he continued to say nothing.

I wasn't the calm and cool woman I used to be. My palms were sweaty, and the palpitations in my chest rocked my rib cage. I was actually nervous around this man when I had no reason to be. "Good morning."

His hand slid into my hair, and he pulled me close. His strong arm wrapped around my waist and tugged me into him. His lips lowered to mine, and he kissed me, his mouth gently embracing my lips. He breathed into me a few times, his fingers lightly fisting my hair as though he didn't care if he messed it up before I walked out the door.

As if a spell had been cast over me, I was paralyzed by that touch. There was no better feeling than being kissed by this man. No other guy had embraced me this way, like I was the most important thing in the world to him. Hades made me feel loved without saying those three little words.

After he pulled away, he released my hair. "You aren't leaving."

"I have work...so do you."

"I only work when I want to. And I definitely don't want to."

When he looked at me like that, the last thing I wanted to do was leave the sanctuary of our bedroom and go into the public eye. I wanted to stay right here and let this man do whatever he wanted to me.

Hades reached his hand up my back until he found the top of my zipper. He slowly pulled it down until the fabric came loose and fell to the floor. He unclasped my bra with a slight movement of his fingertips. His eyes never left mine. "Get your ass back in bed."

After a few days of practically being tied to the bedpost, I was finally able to return to work. Now that I'd stopped thinking about Maddox, I was able to get a lot more work done. My mind wasn't afraid that he would jump around the corner and grab me. Sleeping with Hades seemed to reset my mental state.

It gave me a new start.

I took care of most matters for the hotel and even had a few meetings with the board. I wasn't thrilled the Tuscan Rose was still infiltrated by the country's most notorious criminals, the leaders of organized crime, but I was helpless to fight it. So I let it be.

I'd just finished a meeting with the board in the conference room when Hades quietly stepped inside. He always made the most subtle entrances, but no matter how quiet he was, his presence was so loud. His power permeated the air around him. You could practically feel it.

In a deep blue suit with a matching tie, he stood tall and muscular, with his hands in his pockets. His eyes glanced at the men in their seats before his gaze settled on me. He gave me that dark and dangerous stare, like I was his next victim.

But I wanted to be his next victim.

We still hadn't said more than a few words to each other. It seemed like our relationship had solidified so words were unnecessary for us to communicate.

As the men filed out, they shook hands with Hades and exchanged a few words. They congratulated him on the baby and made small talk about golf and wine. Once the last man was out of the room, Hades slowly stalked to me.

I stacked up my things and placed them on the edge of the

table. I actually avoided eye contact with him sometimes because that stare was too potent. It made me feel like I was under a magnifying glass.

He came up behind me and wrapped his arms around my waist. His hands rested on my small stomach, and he pressed a kiss to my neck.

Bumps formed on my arms, and I suddenly felt hot and cold at the same time. My nipples pierced through my bra and dress, but I also felt the sweat start to bead on my skin. My physiology was completely different because of him. His love had changed my chemical composition, made me into a whole new woman.

His hands moved to my hips, and he slowly turned me around. When we were face-to-face, he pulled me closer and placed a kiss on the corner of my mouth.

Just that simple touch made me want to rip off his clothes and take him on the desk. He made my thoughts irrational, made everything sexualized. I'd always been satisfied with our physical relationship, but now it felt so much better.

He looked into my eyes with that masculine stare. "Have dinner with me." He never asked me questions anymore. He just told me what to do.

But the odd thing was, I liked it. That wasn't me at all. "Alright."

He grabbed the materials sitting on the desk and carried them for me. It was easy for him to hold the binder and laptop in a single grasp so he could hold my hand with his and guide me back to my office.

After he placed everything on my desk, we went outside and got into his car. He always opened the door for me and helped me inside, even before I was pregnant. Then he drove to the restaurant.

We went inside and were seated at a private table off to the side. It was European cuisine, a French-style menu. The waiter was at attention instantly, and Hades ordered a glass of wine for himself and a water for me.

After glancing at the menu, he set it down and stared at me.

My eyes roamed over the selections, but I was aware of his hot gaze. I could feel it burn into me, feel that mix of possession and obsession. It was so distracting that I lifted my gaze to meet his. "Know what you're getting?"

He didn't answer.

I looked at the menu again and decided on a salad. Once I put the menu down, the waiter ran back over. He took our order and our menus and then disappeared.

Hades returned to his favorite hobby and stared at me.

I wanted to hold his gaze just to prove a point, but I couldn't match his intensity. My eyes trailed to the watch on his wrist. Every day when he got ready, he put it back on instead of making a different selection. He normally wore a different watch every day, just the way women wore different necklaces and bracelets to match their outfits. "You don't have to wear it every day…"

He absentmindedly adjusted the watch on his wrist. "I know."

I lifted my eyes to meet his.

"It's my favorite."

"Why?"

He moved his hands back to the table and pulled his wineglass closer. "Because my wife gave it to me."

I felt a flush in my cheeks, the first time I'd showed a visible sign of embarrassment. My own husband made me feel like a shy schoolgirl. Which was ridiculous because I was having his son. There were no secrets between us. "I'm glad you like it."

"I love it."

We hadn't told each other we loved one another since that night. It didn't seem like he regretted it; he was just selective when he said it. I stared at his fingers for a moment before I lifted my gaze to meet his again.

"And I love you…so fucking much." He kept his voice low so no one could overhear our conversation. His eyes showed his masculine intensity, like he was reminding me that I was his.

As if I'd ever forget. I'd never said those words out loud to him. I'd never said them out loud to anybody. I said I hated marriage and didn't believe in love, but now I was head over heels in love with my own husband. I felt like a whole different person. "I love you too…" It felt strange to say those words out loud, to let that confession leave my lips. But it also felt so right. "When I gave you that watch, I was so scared. I wasn't sure if you would feel the same way." We used to have long conversations before his birthday, but lately, it'd been nothing but kisses and sex. It seemed like we were ready to move forward in this new relationship.

"Then why did you tell me?"

I was still in my chair because I couldn't think of a response. Truth be told, I didn't know why I'd done it. If he said nothing in return, it would be awkward for a long time. It had already been awkward enough at the time.

He answered for me. "Because you knew I loved you."

My eyes focused on his.

"You've known it for a long time."

My mouth suddenly felt dry, so I swallowed and felt my throat tighten.

"When I traded places with you, I thought that would be the end. I gave up my life for yours because I'd rather be beaten to death and left to rot in a field than suffer the idea of what was happening to you. I wouldn't have done that unless I was hopelessly in love with you." He held my gaze without fear, unashamed to express such raw emotions. "But to be honest, I've loved you much longer than that."

Feelings like these would normally terrify me, but I wanted to know more. I wanted to know how deep his rivers ran. "How long?"

There was a long pause before he answered. "You go first."

Giving an answer felt daunting. "I don't know…"

"You do know. Answer me." He kept his voice low, but his tone was dictatorial.

"I'm not sure. It started off slow…like a small fire before it erupted and consumed an entire forest. It started as a little thought in my brain, but as it continued to grow, it became undeniable. It honestly feels like I woke up one day and I was in love with you. It just took me a long time to understand that's what I was feeling."

"And when did it start?"

My eyes stared into my water glass. "Months ago. I guess when I saw you in the hospital. But sometimes I wonder if I felt this way a long time ago and didn't realize it then either."

His expression didn't change after he heard my confession. It was controlled and stoic…like he was in a meeting with someone he didn't trust. He didn't blink as he digested what I'd just said.

"Your turn."

He grabbed his glass and took a drink before he told me. "Sofia, I've loved you forever."

My heart started to race a little faster.

"I loved you shortly after we met. I loved you when we were together. I loved you when we were apart. I loved you when I asked you to marry me...both times." He looked into my gaze without fear. "It feels good to tell you that. It feels good to tell you the truth without scaring you away. It feels so good to love a woman and have her love me back."

Hades walked in the door in his running shorts, his chest and neck covered in sweat. He pulled his earbuds out of his ears and then wiped his forehead with the back of his arm. He moved into his closet and took off his shoes and socks and dropped his bottoms before he stepped into the bedroom completely naked.

I was sitting in bed in his t-shirt, reading a baby book. I forgot the paragraph I'd just read because the sight of him, his muscles pumped with blood, was incredibly distracting. My fingers shut the book absentmindedly. "How was your workout?" It was nice to see him hitting the gym again. He'd been too injured to do anything more than physical therapy. Now he was getting strong again, lifting weights and building muscle.

He didn't answer my question. He came to the bed and lifted up my shirt so he could kneel down and kiss my bump everywhere. His large hands cupped either side of my belly, and he loved the son growing inside me.

For nearly two weeks, we'd spent our time in newlywed

bliss. We'd been married for over six months now, but it felt like we were starting over. We made love through the night, and whenever we needed a break, we spent our time talking about things that we never talked about before. With every passing day, I grew more in love with the man who had loved me for so long. How did I not see what was right in front of me? How did I not fall madly in love with him at first sight? There was no better man in this world, and I still didn't understand how he was mine.

After he finished kissing my belly, he placed a soft kiss on my mouth. He tasted salty from the sweat, but it was still a good kiss. He righted himself and stood to his full height before he gently replaced the shirt over my stomach. "I'm gonna get in the shower."

"You want me to join you?"

A slight smile emerged on his lips. "Always."

I followed him into the bathroom, and we got under the water together. I rubbed soap onto his chest and arms, watching the suds turn into bubbles and drip down his hard body. The water followed the rivers in his stomach, dripping all the way down his powerful thighs and toned calves. There were scars on his body that would be there for the rest of his life, but that didn't detract from his perfection. In fact, it made him even more perfect.

He rubbed the soap onto my tummy. He used to be infatuated with my tits and ass, but now all he cared about was my pregnant belly. When we were in bed together, he liked having me on top because he liked to stare at my stomach as I bounced up and down. He was clearly excited to be a father, even though he seemed like the kind of man that might not be interested in settling down.

Life had been good these past few weeks, so good that I forgot about reality, forgot that we still had a problem to address. Now that my son would be part of our family in a few months, I had to protect him with my life. That meant Maddox needed to be eliminated…for good. Hades had not mentioned his vengeance once since his birthday. "Hades?"

He lifted his gaze to mine.

"Have you figured out how to take care of him?" I assumed he would know who I was talking about. I hated saying his name; it seemed to give him more power.

Hades stared at me for several heartbeats with his hands still on my belly. "No."

I couldn't keep the disappointment out of my face. "Well, you need to. I can't raise a son in a world where he exists." I knew Hades would do anything for me, and it was ridiculous to be upset with him for not taking care of this problem sooner. If it were that simple, he would've done it already. But I wanted this finished so I knew for sure I never had to worry again.

"I'll take care of it. I promise."

"I know, but I want him gone now. What's taking so long?"

His eyes drifted down again, and a loud sigh escaped his lips. He probably didn't want to talk about it, especially when we were having a nice moment under the water. "It's complicated. He's hard to track down. I've found a way to lure him out, but he hasn't shown his face yet. But he will."

"And you think this will work?"

He nodded. "It's only a matter of time."

"And when he does show up, you'll kill him?"

His hand cupped my cheek. "Yes. I will torture him for what he did to you, for what he did to me. And I will make sure he's dead and gone." His hand slowly slid down to my neck. "But don't worry about him. The only thing you should be worrying about is our son. He's my problem…not yours."

23

HADES

My PHONE LIT UP ON THE NIGHTSTAND WITH A TEXT message. It was Damien. *We need to talk. Ash and I are at the bar.*

I glanced at the time and realized it was almost midnight.

Sofia was cuddled into my side, her face in the crook of my neck and her arm at my waist.

I didn't want to leave my wife, but I knew this was important. I slid out of bed and entered the walk-in closet to put on jeans, a t-shirt, and a jacket. The watch Sofia gave me was clasped around my wrist, and I put on my boots before I crept across the floor to the door.

Sofia realized I wasn't there as she reached out her hand to feel me beside her. With her eyes still closed, she continued to feel the sheets until my absence stirred her from sleep. She opened her eyes and sat up in bed, searching for me with squinted eyes. When she realized I was in front of the door, she sighed. "Where are you going?" She ran her fingers through her hair to keep it out of her face.

I came back to the bed and sat on the edge. "I need to meet the guys."

"Right now?"

"Yeah. I gotta go."

She did the one thing I couldn't resist. She reached out and grabbed the front of my shirt. She yanked me toward her, bringing our lips together for a kiss.

I loved it when she did that. She'd been doing it since the night we met, and it was a sign of her passion. If killing Maddox weren't so important, I would sink on top of her and never leave.

I kissed her back and lowered her to the bed. But then my brain took control, and I sat up again. "I'll be home soon."

Her eyes filled with disappointment. "I worry when you go out late like this…"

"I'll be fine, I promise."

She looked like she wanted to argue with me, but she silenced her disapproval. "Wake me up when you come home."

"Alright."

"I mean it. You always say you'll do it, but you never do."

That was because I didn't want to wake her up. "Okay." I

leaned down and gave her a kiss before I got up from the bed and headed to the door.

Leaving my pregnant wife was the hardest thing I ever had to do. She was in bed, begging me not to leave, and she had no idea I would rather be with her than anywhere else in the world. I didn't want to sneak off in the middle of the night to sit in a bar while women bought me drinks. It reminded me of what my life was like before her...and that wasn't something I wanted to think about.

I got in my car and drove a few blocks until I parked out front. I walked inside and found the guys in our usual booth. They were both single men, loving every opportunity to get out of the house and land pussy. Not that either of them had to try.

The waitress already knew my drink, so she came by and dropped off a scotch before giving us privacy. It was loud inside, the bass thumping from the speakers, drowning out conversations everyone was having. The noise was obnoxious, and I started to feel like an old man who never wanted to leave my home.

Why would I when my whole world was there?

Damien and I hadn't spoken since our argument in the bar weeks ago. He'd told me off and very coldly put me in my place. He used to be apologetic, wanting us to repair our relationship, but now it seemed like he hated me as much as I hated him. He turned to me, his dislike obvious in his eyes. "Bad night?"

I took a drink. "The opposite. So this better be important."

Damien cast me a glare. "Trust me, I wouldn't call unless it was important. The less I see your fuck face, the better."

Ash glanced back and forth between us, clearly confused by the bitter exchange. Damien probably hadn't told him about our last argument. And I certainly hadn't either. "Let's focus, boys."

If this were the olden days, I would tell Damien that the woman I loved, loved me too. But those days were gone. "You found him?"

Damien shook his head. "No. But we know exactly where to find his biggest distributor. The shipping company takes his drugs directly into Scotland and then to England. We know exactly where they're going to be tomorrow night. Once we take them out, Maddox will be left with nothing."

Ash nodded. "We could take out all those guys. Easy."

This was exactly the news I needed. My own wife was disappointed in me for not getting her the vengeance she deserved, the vengeance our family deserved. It killed me to look her in the eye and see her fear. It killed me to know that I didn't murder the man who raped my wife. I had to get this fucker at any cost. "Good. We hit them hard tomorrow night. We keep one asshole alive to tell Maddox what we did. He'll be forced to surrender, and when he does, I'll kill him." My hand tightened into a fist because I imagined my fingers curling around his neck. I would break every bone in his body and remember the way he screamed.

Damien drank from his glass and didn't look at me again.

Ash seemed to be the mediator between the two of us. "With my men and yours, this should be straightforward."

Damien finished the rest of his glass before he stood up. He pulled out cash from his wallet and threw it on the table. "I'll see you tomorrow." He walked away from our table and exited the bar.

Ash stared at the door for a while before he turned his gaze back on to me. He then stared at me for a while, giving me that obnoxious look he'd been giving me since we were kids. He was reading me, figuring out if something got under my skin. "If you wait too long, you'll lose your chance altogether."

I slowly turned my head his way, my blood starting to boil in anger. I gave him a cold look.

Ash didn't take back what he said. "Good friends are hard to find, man."

"Yes," I said through gritted teeth. "And I have yet to find one."

He relaxed against the leather seat, his arm draping over the back. He shook his head slightly, showing his disappointment. "This is one of those situations where you'll forget what you're angry about ten years from now. But you won't forget how shitty you feel not having that person in your life anymore. He said he was sorry. Let it go...before he can't let it go."

My temper flared. "Before he can't let what go? Everything is his fault. My wife was raped because of him."

"No," he said calmly. "Your wife was raped because Maddox is an asshole. There was no way Damien could've predicted that. I'm not saying the guy is a saint, but we both know he would never intentionally cause you harm."

"Doesn't fucking matter. He didn't listen to me...twice."

"Yes, he's a fucking dumbass. But again, he didn't do it on purpose. You really think you would ever listen to anybody?"

I shook my head because the answer was no. "That's because no one knows what the fuck they're doing... including him."

Ash dropped the conversation, letting the silence simmer for a while. He glanced around the bar and looked at the pretty girls in their short dresses before he turned back to me. "I'm just looking out for you. The two of you have been friends a long time. He made a mistake, and he apologized. Let it go."

I just got my brother back into my life, and I didn't want to push him away. "If you'd ever loved a woman, you would understand."

"You killed our father point-blank, and I forgave you. You need to forgive this."

I let a cold laugh escape my lips. "Not the same thing. Not even close."

"Exactly," Ash said. "It's murder. It's much worse."

I wanted to blow up at my brother, but I managed to calm myself down. "I want nothing to do with him. When this is over, I'm done with him."

He didn't have another argument. He turned quiet, like he'd finally accepted my decision. "The person who suffered the most is Sofia. She forgave him." He looked me in the eye for several seconds. "If she can do that, so can you."

When I came home, I was in a bad mood.

I was relieved I finally had a concrete plan to get rid of that cockroach, but I was irritated that my brother didn't understand my position. He loved Sofia in his own way, so I expected him to be on my side. Choosing Damien felt like a betrayal. I shouldn't have to explain myself. I shouldn't have to be patronized.

I got undressed in the closet, then came back to bed. My beautiful wife was asleep and waiting for me, pregnant with my first son, and I should be grateful she was there. The anger and resentment should melt off me like sweat. But I was stiff and rigid, the booze unable to freeze my pain.

I lay beside her without waking her up. I wanted to close my eyes and go to sleep, but I'd made a promise to her and I had to keep it. I turned over and pressed a kiss to her shoulder. "Baby, I'm home."

It took her a couple seconds to understand because her mind was foggy. But when her eyes opened and focused on me, a dreamy smile moved across her lips and she cuddled into my side like she hadn't seen me in weeks.

My arms wrapped around her, and I placed a kiss to her forehead.

"I'm glad you're home."

I ran my fingers through her hair and inhaled her scent. It was preferable to the smell of cheap perfume in the bar, the fumes from the drinks. The spot next to her was my safe place, my cloud nine. "Yeah, I'm glad I'm home too."

She must've picked up on the slight annoyance in my voice because she pulled back so she could look at my face. She shared my home and my bed, so she was around my moods all the time. She could pick up on subtle cues other people wouldn't notice. "What's wrong?"

"Nothing. Go back to sleep." I pressed another kiss to her forehead so she would relax and drift off.

She wouldn't let it go. She propped herself up on one elbow so she could look down on me. "You can talk to me about anything." Her fingers lightly touched my chest, trying to bring me into a relaxed state.

"I know. I just don't want to."

Her voice became a little more forceful. "Well, you're going to." She leaned down and kissed me on the mouth. "Right now." When she pulled away, she gave me an unflinching stare, waiting for me to get the weight off my chest.

I couldn't deny her, especially when she was so cute and demanding. "Damien and I aren't getting along, and Ash thinks I need to forgive him…before it's too late." My eyes shifted to the ceiling because I didn't want to see her reaction. I just wanted to close my eyes and go to sleep.

She propped her head on her palm and ran her fingers up and down my chest. She didn't throw her opinion out at me right away, letting the silence do all the talking. After she'd told me she loved me and I told her I felt the same way, our relationship had changed. We spent less time talking and more time living in the moment with each other. Like we'd both adopted an extra sense for understanding the other, we could communicate just by breathing. That seemed to be what she was doing now…just being with me.

My arm was wrapped around her waist, and my fingers moved under her shirt to feel her bare skin. Being in bed with her was far more comfortable than that leather booth at the bar. I'd rather drink her kisses than a full bottle of scotch.

She whispered in the dark. "Why don't you forgive him?"

My eyes shifted back to hers, to a pair of the most beautiful eyes I'd ever seen. I always looked deep inside them when I made love to her. With my other lovers, I barely gave them that kind of attention. "Because I don't want to."

Her fingers continued to caress me. "I was hoping the two of you would have resolved this by now."

"There's nothing to resolve. Everything that has happened is because of him."

She rested her hand over my heart. "Including this?"

I felt my heartbeat pound against her chest.

"I don't think it's fair to put that kind of burden on Damien. I know what happened to me eats him alive. I know he loves me, would die for me. It's harsh to put all that guilt on him. And besides, the things that happened were terrible, but they brought us closer together."

Maybe she was right, but I still couldn't accept it. "I'm so happy right now, but this with us would've happened no matter what. Justifying what happened to you will never be okay. Maddox was provoked by Damien's stupidity. I don't forgive him. I can't forgive him."

"What if I want you to forgive him?"

Even that wouldn't make a difference. "We identified his biggest distributor at the ports. We're gonna finish them, and then Maddox will crawl out of the shadows. This is almost over…almost."

She didn't seem upset by the change in subject. "Be careful. What I learned from Maddox is that he's unpredictable. Expect the unexpected. Even if it seems like you've won, keep fighting like you lost."

I took her warning seriously, but it also made me sick to my stomach. I hated to imagine what she had been through to make that kind of observation, to know how he tortured her to become so tactical. I had to kill this man for what he did to this wonderful woman. She was innocent and didn't deserve that fate. It was wrong, and no matter what I did, I could never make it right. All I could do was kill him, and hope that would be enough.

"I'm always willing to help. If there's anything I can do to finish this, I'm happy to do it."

I didn't want her anywhere near him ever again. It was my job to protect her. It was one of the reasons she'd agreed to marry me in the first place. "I can handle it, baby."

She returned her head to my shoulder and cuddled into my side. "I know you can."

I left the house in the early afternoon.

Sofia wasn't ready to let me go. She kept looking at me like I might not come back. Those big beautiful eyes were full of worry, and she wore her vulnerability like a second skin. She kept touching me, grabbing my arm or my shoulder because she wanted to feel me as much as she could before I left.

I'd be lying if I said I didn't enjoy this. It was the best feeling in the world, to watch the woman I loved love me like this. I was the only man in her heart, and until I was safe, she would constantly worry about me. I was her whole world. It was what I'd always wanted. "I'll be back tomorrow." My hands cupped her cheeks, and I brought her face close to mine. My thumb brushed over her bottom lip, and I treasured the sight of her beautiful face.

"Please be careful."

I told her to stay in the house until I came home. Under no circumstances was she allowed to leave. I'd learned my lesson after Maddox had ruined my life. "Everything will be okay. I've got lots of men with me, and this isn't my first time."

"Well, I'm still terrified. We need you to come home."

I loved the way she referred to both her and Andrew, like he was already here. I knew we would have another son, so I would survive this. Or maybe that prophecy was no longer set in stone because I had broken the curse. "I'll be back before you know it."

She sighed deeply. "Okay." She moved into my chest and rested her cheek against my body. Her hands moved up my chest as she held on to me tightly.

I held her against me, my chin resting on her head. The car was waiting for me downstairs and I needed to go, but I wanted to be there for her for as long as she needed. I wanted to comfort my wife and be everything she required.

She eventually pulled away and looked at me. "I love you."

My hand slid into her hair, and I inhaled a deep breath when I heard those words. Music to my ears and pleasure to my heart, it was the most beautiful thing I'd ever heard someone say. It wasn't just the words she uttered, but it was the emotion in her voice, the sincerity in her eyes. It was the visible way she loved me, the way she meant it from the bottom of her soul. I'd dreamed of this for so long, pictured myself telling her how I felt years ago. If I had it my way, she would've been my wife a long time ago. "I love you too."

Ash and I sat in the back seat of the SUV at the docks. Damien was in another car, but we could communicate with him through our comms system. Things were so tense between us that he didn't even want to be in my vicinity.

The feeling was mutual.

It was pitch black outside, and the ships at the dock were dark because no one was on board. We had taken over security and infiltrated with our own guys so we would know exactly when Maddox's team was about to arrive.

An hour later, a large ship approached the dock, and two men popped out to secure it. At the same time, one of my guys spoke in my ear. "The truck is approaching."

I turned to Ash and gave him a nod. "Any moment now."

Ash had an assault rifle around his shoulders, and he held it in front of him at the ready to do what was necessary when the moment came.

The truck stopped, and a few men hopped out and opened

the back. From our camera feed, we could see that it was completely stuffed with meth. There had to be several tons on board, ready to be shipped to the rest of Europe.

Looking at his product pissed me off. It was inferior to mine, which just annoyed me more.

I gave the signal to my team. "Let's go."

The bodies were piled on the concrete, and the truck full of drugs had been driven right into the water. I wanted to make sure Maddox couldn't recover it so he would be at a complete loss. The men on the ship had been executed, and my men would make sure they were stuffed in oil drums to be dropped deep into the ocean.

Only one guy remained. On his knees with his hands in the air, he shook on the spot. It was dark outside, but it was clear he had a wet outline on the front of his jeans. The pussy pissed himself like a little boy. "I got kids. Come on."

My wife had a husband, but that didn't stop Maddox. "Everyone else is dead. You think there's any possibility you're gonna get out of this alive?"

He dropped his gaze and began to shake more. He even began to cry.

I wanted to shoot him in the head for being such a coward. When I'd thought Maddox was going to kill me, I held my head high and didn't give in. He beat me with a bat, and not once did I make a single sound.

Ash sat beside me, his arms folded over his chest. He looked bored.

"You know what? I will let you go."

The man looked up at me, astonished.

"Just tell me where I can find Maddox."

His face turned white. "I don't know where he is…"

I cocked my gun. "Yes, you do."

"Even if I did, I can't tell you. Maybe you'll spare my life now, but he won't spare mine later."

I held my gun at my side. "You're taking a gamble, I get it. But if you tell me where he's at, and I kill him, no one's coming after you."

He lowered his hands to his thighs and considered what I said. There was a small look of hope in his eyes, a dream he might be able to get out of this. But then that shine slowly faded away. "No." He shook his head as he gave his final answer. "No one can kill him. No one."

Every single one of his men refused to roll on him. It was the kind of loyalty I couldn't explain. Maddox was a psychotic madman. How could he scare these men so deeply? "You should've put your money on me." I raised my gun, aimed between the eyes, and pulled the trigger.

He fell back with a thud, his blood everywhere.

Ash didn't react at all, not even to the sound of the loud gunshot as it echoed off all the cargo bins. "It's like they're robots."

"He must have dirt on all of them. Must keep track of all their affairs, their debts. He probably promised to ruin their legacy if they compromised him before they died." Maddox was thorough and paranoid. He left nothing to chance... which was why I couldn't get rid of him.

Damien walked over to us, mostly looking at Ash and avoiding me. "Maddox is officially finished. We could either wait for him to call, or we could call him first." He turned his eyes on me. "What do you wanna do?"

I clicked the safety on my gun and stuffed it into the back of my jeans. "I need to think about it."

Damien continued to stare at me, like he had something to say. A full minute passed, and his gaze seemed to become more formidable. "I'm the one who tracked down every distributor. I'm the one who tailed all the guys. I'm the one who was out every night trying to get this shit done." Like that was supposed to be enough to earn my forgiveness, he waited for me to acknowledge his sacrifice.

It only pissed me off more. "Congratulations. You finally did your job."

24

SOFIA

I couldn't sleep.

Knowing he might die tonight made it impossible for me to relax. He had Damien and Ash along with the rest of his men, but that wasn't enough for me. Until I knew he was safe and unharmed, I would sit in the dark with my hand on my stomach, waiting to hear news about my husband.

I kept glancing at my phone to make sure it wasn't on Do Not Disturb.

It was two-thirty in the morning…and still nothing.

I considered calling him, because he'd told me I could. But I didn't want to bother him when he had more important things to worry about. And if he didn't answer, that would only stress me out even more.

It was crazy to think that this man had meant nothing to me at one point in time. He was just a good lay, man candy. But now, he was the love of my life, the man I dreamed of when I went to sleep. I couldn't lose him. I just couldn't.

Thankfully, my phone started to ring with his name on the screen. I took the call right away and breathed into the phone. "Are you okay?"

"Yes, baby. I'm fine."

I clutched my chest and breathed harder into the phone. I was so relieved I could barely catch my breath. "Where are you?"

"Just finished cleaning up at the docks. We'll be home by late morning."

I still wasn't sure if I could sleep until he came home. "Okay, are the guys okay?"

"Yeah, Ash and Damien are fine."

"Good. Tell them I said hi."

He didn't respond to that. "I gotta go. I just called because I knew you'd worry."

I felt like an overprotective mother who couldn't let her kids grow up, but I didn't care if I was overdramatic. I wanted my husband to come back in the same condition as when he left. "Thank you. I'll see you when you get home."

Before he got off the phone, he had one more thing to say. "I love you." It was the first time he'd said it to me over the phone, the first time he'd said it to me in the way couples usually did. It was so normal. But it was such a lovely thing to hear, such a comfort since I was home alone.

I loved my husband so much, I could barely take it. I didn't know how this happened, how I fell so madly in love with a man. I'd been detached my entire life, never clinging to any man I met. But now I was obsessed with my husband. "I love you too…"

He came home just before noon. In the same clothes he'd worn when he left, he looked the same as he stepped inside. There were no new bruises or scars, and no signs of blood or injury. The only difference was he seemed exhausted.

I ran into his arms right away and wrapped my arms around his neck. I was still in his t-shirt because I didn't get ready for the day. I'd been too stressed to sleep or shower. "I'm so happy you're home."

He lifted me from the floor and held me so we were eye level with each other. He hadn't been able to pick me up in a long time, but now he was strong enough to lift me effortlessly. His large hands gripped my ass as he carried me back to the bed. His lips moved to mine, and he kissed me as he held me in the air. He should be tired and eager for a shower, but he cared more about curing my broken heart. "I told you I would come back."

"I know. But seeing your face is so much better than hearing your words."

He studied my gaze for a while, looking into my eyes like he could do it forever. "You didn't sleep."

"How could I, when you weren't next to me?" I'd never committed to a man before, but now I was the clingiest woman the world had ever seen. My priorities had changed, and the most important things to me were this man and the little boy we'd made together. It was crazy how so much could change in the blink of an eye.

His eyes softened slightly, so subtly it was hardly noticeable. My husband was a strong man, the strong and silent type, the kind that thrived in the shadows and winced in the light. That was why I was so attracted to him in the first place. So when I saw him soften for me, have emotion for me, it spoke volumes. His hand moved to my cheek, and he brought our foreheads together. His fingers moved down to my neck, and he lightly pressed into me as he held me. "I'm here now. And soon, this will all be over."

I knew Hades would get rid of Maddox. I had no doubt he would give me the revenge I deserved. I just needed to be patient a little longer, accept his absence a little longer. This would come to an end soon, and we would never have to think about it again.

After he pressed a kiss to my forehead, he released me and stepped back. "I'm gonna shower and get some sleep."

It was almost noon, so he'd been up for almost two days. I wasn't surprised by his exhaustion.

He stripped off his jacket and tossed it on the chair for

Helena to grab later. His watch came undone, and he set it on the nightstand instead of in his special drawer. He wore the same watch every single day…the watch I gave him.

Our relationship had changed so much, and he never put me down for feeling differently. He reciprocated my affections and never made me feel stupid for putting my heart on the line. That made me more secure, made me more loved. "Can I join you?"

He lifted his gaze and looked at me, his jaw tight but his eyes soft. "Always."

We sat in the doctor's office and waited for the results to come in. I sat in the chair with my hand on my slight stomach, unafraid of what we would find out. I knew my son was alive and well inside me. I could feel it; I could sense it.

I could also tell my husband was stressed.

He sat in his jeans and jacket, his eyes on the opposite wall without really looking at anything. His eyes were open and unblinking, and it was clear he had a million thoughts on his mind. He hadn't been very affectionate or talkative lately. I knew it had nothing to do with me, but I worried anyway.

"Andrew is fine."

When Hades heard my voice, he slowly turned to me and

met my gaze. It took him a few seconds to process what I'd just said. "I know, baby."

My hand moved to his on his thigh. "Then why are you so upset?"

He faced the wall again. "I'm not."

"I can tell something is on your mind."

After a few seconds, he sighed. He slowly turned back to me. "I don't think a doctor's office is an appropriate place for this conversation."

"No place is appropriate."

He was quiet for a while before he answered. "I expected to hear from Maddox by now. I hit his distributors hard and took out most of his men."

"He's probably just stubborn."

He shook his head slightly. "Maybe. Maybe not."

I squeezed his hand. "I'm sure he's running out of options, and he'll surrender soon."

His hand finally came to life, and he slipped his fingers through mine. "Let's not worry about that now. This should be a happy moment for us."

"It is." I leaned into him and rested my face on his shoulder. "Our son is healthy, and you'll be getting rid of Maddox soon. We'll have the life that we want...soon enough."

He turned his head my way and pressed a kiss to my forehead. "Yes, we will."

Hades was out of the house, so I texted Damien. *How are you?* As time went by, I heard from him less and less. He used to be a big part of our lives, and now he'd ceased to exist. He wasn't just a friend of my husband...he was a friend of mine too.

Shitty.

I could hear the sarcasm in his reply. *Damien, I'm being serious.*

So am I. Shitty.

Are you with Hades right now?

No.

I picked up the phone and decided to call him instead.

When he answered, he was just as annoyed. "Did you need something?"

I ignored his assholeness. "I just want to see how my friend is doing."

He sighed loudly. "Tensions are high. Shit is taking forever. I'm not getting laid. So yeah, I'm not doing too well. And since Hades and I are enemies, that means you and I are enemies too."

I refused to take that literally. "No matter what's going on between the two of you, it doesn't make us lesser friends. And you two are not enemies."

"When this is all over, I doubt I'll ever see him again. I doubt I'll ever want to see him again. And I know that feeling is mutual."

It was crazy to see how far they'd fallen. I used to think this whole thing would blow over, but now I realized it was here to stay. Hades couldn't forget what Damien did, and Damien grew resentful of his best friend's coldness. Things seemed to be getting worse by the day, not better. "I hope you two find your way back to each other."

"This isn't a fairy tale. This is real shit. It's not going to change."

25

HADES

WHEN I WALKED THROUGH THE DOOR, I COULD FEEL THE hostility in the room. I'd been living with my wife for almost a year, and I could read her moods like words on a page. I could feel her joy in her smile, feel her rage in her posture. I took one look at her and knew an unpleasant conversation was about to follow.

She stood in jeans and a tight t-shirt, her slight belly stretching the fabric right in the front. Her eyelashes were thick with makeup, and her lips were plump from the shade of lipstick she chose. She was so beautiful, it was sometimes easy to forget she was angry.

"Looks like I did something bad." I walked up to her, unintimidated by the ferocity in her eyes. Instead of being deterred by that look, I was intrigued. Nothing she did could scare me off. Every action she made only made me want her more.

Her arms were across her chest, and she loosened them and

placed her hands on her hips. "I'm only going to say this one more time. I hope you listen to me because you're running out of time."

I already knew what she was going to say.

"Make things right with Damien. This isn't worth losing him over."

Maybe she didn't understand how much I had suffered. Maybe she didn't understand I'd cried myself to sleep every night she was gone. I was still haunted by what happened to her, and twenty years could pass and I'd feel the exact same way. Damien could have stolen from me, and I wouldn't have cared. In this line of business, nothing could be personal. Everything was business.

But my wife was different.

My soul mate was different.

She studied my gaze, disappointment flooding her features when she read my stubborn look.

I didn't need to give a verbal response. The look on my face was more than enough.

She dropped her gaze and gave a slight shake of her head. "Fine."

I truly hoped that was the end of this conversation.

"You're going to regret this, but I obviously can't change your mind."

I was sitting at the bank when one of my guys called me. There was a production issue in the lab, so all processes were put on indefinite hold. The cause of the delay was unclear, and since I was so involved in every aspect of my business, I wanted to participate in finding the solution.

In my black suit, I walked down the hallway and entered Damien's office. We both had become experts at silent hatred. We retained a sense of professionalism, but we constantly showed our distaste for each other through our gazes. I still looked at him like his betrayal had just happened yesterday. "Production has been shut down at the lab."

"Yeah, I just got the call."

"I'll go down and take care of it." We hadn't decided how we'd split this business when this was over. It belonged to us equally, but it would be impossible to divide a business in two. It would also be impossible to run it without seeing each other on a weekly basis. I could barely stand to look at his face now. He looked like he wanted to punch me every second of the day. We couldn't do this much longer.

"I'm going too. Sounds like a shitshow down there."

I didn't argue because he could do whatever he wanted. I turned away because I wasn't waiting for him. We were going to the same place, but we would take separate rides. We were business partners on paper but adversaries in real life. It was sad that our lives had ended up this way, but there was nothing we could do to change it. He stood by his decisions, and I would stand by mine.

When I stepped off the elevator and entered the lab, I immediately knew something wasn't right. Damien was already there, standing with sagging shoulders with his head tilted to the ground.

All the lab equipment was turned off, and the usual steam that rose to the ceiling was nonexistent. It ordinarily smelled like chemicals, but that potent smell was absent because production had been halted for hours.

My men were on the opposite side of the room, huddled together like livestock on a farm. A couple men circled them, keeping them quiet without drawing their guns. There were a lot of foreign faces in the space, people who had no business being there.

One of those faces belonged to Maddox.

It quickly dawned on me that this was all a setup. My men lured both of us here so there would be no witnesses, not a single sound anyone could hear. It was a perfect place to provoke me...on my turf, where I would least expect it.

My heart rate quickened and there was a shot of adrenaline in my blood, but I didn't cave to the fear. I kept a blank stare like I didn't give a damn that Maddox was there at all. It was obvious Damien had been blindsided too.

I stepped farther into the room and discreetly counted the number of men I was up against. There had to be several dozen, all armed and all loyal. All I had was a knife inside my suit jacket. Damien usually had a pistol on him, but that was pretty much useless at the moment.

My eyes moved to Maddox as I approached the center of the room. Without all the apparatus working, it was actually really quiet down here in the basement. No sounds from the outside world to puncture the concrete walls. We were underground and far away from civilization.

Within seconds, I felt the hostility rip me from the inside out. The vein in my forehead enlarged as more adrenaline was released into my system. My heart started to pound so sporadically, I thought I might have a heart attack. There was so much pain inside my chest, so much unspent rage that I didn't know what to do with it. Looking at those blue eyes made my hand shake and my shoulders go rigid.

All I could see was red.

This man did unspeakable things to my wife...the woman I loved...the mother of my child.

I wanted to kill him with my bare hands, rip out his eyeballs, and shove them up his ass. The longer I stared at him, the less I could resist the urge. Damien and I were outnumbered and we needed to use logic to talk ourselves out of this mess, but all I wanted to do was rip out Maddox's throat and step on it.

I continued to move toward him, lost in the blood lust that had taken control of my body.

Maddox smiled like this was exactly what he wanted. His blue eyes were charismatic, and his boyish smile made him look innocent. He was a psychopath, using my hatred as fuel for his amusement. "You clean up good, Hades."

My feet moved quicker, and I launched myself at his face. My hand balled into a fist, and I punched him so hard he flew backward and landed on the concrete with a skid. My knuckles ached as I smashed into bone. I could feel his blood drip on my hands because the impact had been so profound. I never knew my body could unleash such vigorous force. I thought I'd lost my innate strength, but my body seemed to put itself together just for this moment.

Maddox stayed on the ground for a moment as his body absorbed the shock of the hit. Blood dripped from his cheek and his nose, down his chin onto his neck. He wiped his nose with the back of his forearm and admired the red liquid that leaked from his body. He released a light chuckle even though that must've hurt all the way down to his core.

I lunged at him again, but his men grabbed me and pulled me away. I fought against the restraint because I cared about his death more than my own life. It was a biological compulsion, a desperate need to snuff out his life like a flickering candle.

Maddox got to his feet slowly, rejecting the help from his men. He straightened and wiped away another river of blood. "Let him go." His shirt was stained from his wounds, but he continued to smile like this was all a joke. "He's not gonna be able to focus until he gets this out of his system. Let him do what he wants." He waved to his men. "Come on, he deserves it."

After a few seconds of hesitation, his men released me. They slowly backed away and took their time, like they expected Maddox to change his mind.

He should change his mind.

Maddox raised his arms at his sides and beckoned me forward with his fingers. "Take your shot."

This seemed like a trick, a setup to get me where he wanted me. It seemed too good to be true, but then again, Maddox was unpredictable. It was one of his strengths. There was no way to anticipate any meeting with him because you never knew what to expect.

Damien came to my side and gently placed his hand on my shoulder. "I don't know what the fuck is going on, but don't fall for it."

I shoved his hand off my shoulder. "Too late." I lunged at Maddox again and let my fists beat him like a punching bag. I slugged him in the stomach, slammed his face down into my knee, and then punched him in the face so hard, one tooth came loose. His defeated body continued to hit the floor, and I was the one who had to pull him to his feet so I could finish the job. Every hit was an outlet for my agony, a kind of therapy my entire body needed. But I knew the one thing I needed above all was his death.

But I knew he wouldn't give that to me.

Maddox got to his feet again and stepped back with his hands raised. "All right, enough." He grabbed the bottom of his shirt and wiped it across his face to get rid of all the blood. He'd taken a serious beating but shrugged it off like nothing happened. He was just as coherent as ever. "We're even."

Smoke almost exploded from my ears. "Even? No, asshole. Not even close."

Maddox walked closer to me, not the least bit afraid because all his cronies were ready to pull me off if I launched another attack. "Well, we need to get down to business. Your little vendetta can wait."

"Business?" I had no business with this fucking lunatic. The only business we would ever have would be buying a plot to put his body. "The only business I have with you is my vendetta. If you came here expecting me to surrender, I won't. I will not stop until you pay for what you did."

He placed his hands on his hips. "Well, I guess I could pay you for your wife's time."

Within a single snap, I lost my shit. I sprinted into his frame and grabbed his head so I could snap his neck.

He was lucky his men pulled me off so quickly. If they hadn't, I would've gotten him.

"Will you calm the fuck down now? Do I need to let you wail on me a little longer so you'll listen?"

Two of his men held me back by the arms because I could no longer be trusted to stay sane. "If you really want me to listen, let me kill you."

He slowly walked toward me with his hands on his hips. "In my experience, the dead don't say much, and they listen even less. I'm sure you noticed that after you killed my brother." He mentioned the murder of his brother like it was no big deal, like he didn't need vengeance for what I'd done. He was so disassociated from reality. He seemed to operate on a completely different field.

"I hope you aren't expecting an apology."

"I hope you aren't either."

I tried to free myself from my restraint, but it was no use.

Maddox held up his hand, like the gesture was going to soothe me. "This is what we're gonna do. You successfully put me out of business." He brought his hands together and slow clapped. "Congratulations. Now, I need a new partner, someone who has channels all over the world. The Tuscan Rose is really impressive because it's the perfect place for such a complicated network of distributors. I think it's the perfect place for me to settle."

I stared at him with a blank face, unable to process what he was saying because it was so ridiculous. "You really are out of your mind, aren't you?"

"No, you are. What did you think was going to happen when you stripped everything away? You know what they say, destroy one monster and you make a bigger one." He raised both arms and gave a shrug. "I think you and I could work well together. I've always admired you. Why do you think I've kept you alive so long?"

I pushed his men off of me and continued to look Maddox in the eyes. "I'd rather die." I wouldn't work with a man who'd raped my wife. I wouldn't form an alliance with the man who'd nearly beat me to death.

Maddox's face slowly turned serious. "You know what they say. If you can't beat 'em, join 'em. You and I would no longer be enemies, and if we aren't enemies, we all get along real nicely. Your wife is safe, your kid is safe. Sounds like a win-win to me."

"I'd. Rather. Die."

His eyes shifted back and forth as he looked into my face. He held the look for a long time, oscillating between all the different emotions that occupied his body. His hands slid into his front pockets, and his chin tilted toward the ground as he considered my response. "Then I guess I'll have to kill you and Damien right here…and then have some more fun with your wife." He lifted his chin to meet my gaze again, this time his look threatening. "After I kill your son, of course."

I couldn't process the million shocks of rage that flooded my body. Like being electrocuted with a bolt of lightning, my body could barely handle the voltage. I wanted to kill this man more than anything else in the world. I was so livid, I actually couldn't speak. My life meant nothing to me, but my wife meant everything. And my son...I couldn't even go there.

Maddox continued to study me. "Good. You changed your mind."

Once I was reminded of the stakes, I couldn't defy him. I had too much to lose. Provoking him like this was another mistake to add to the pile. I had to protect my family above everything else, even if that meant I had to swallow my pride.

Maddox didn't gloat at his victory. "I think you and I can do great things. We'll be the most powerful men in the drug world. We'll be untouchable." He slowly stepped away from me and motioned for his men to get ready to leave.

I felt like a little bitch that had to listen to his master. I was a free man, but now I was a slave. I was livid when I looked at him, but now I was sick to my stomach. I should've spent the last few years hunting him down to kill him. Or I should have walked away from this life a long time ago.

"Hades?"

I turned my gaze back to him.

"I would never cause harm to you, your family, or anyone you care about. But if you try to kill me, you better succeed. Because I'll take your wife and fuck her in the ass until she begs me to kill her."

Everyone left, and now it was just the two of us.

Alone. In the lab.

Neither one of us ever spent any extended time in here. I was there on occasion, when lab techs got killed and I had to cook to stay on production. Damien did the same thing when needed, but I was much better at it.

Now we were both there for a whole new reason.

We had been assaulted in our own territory, stabbed in the back because we were too busy looking forward. While we were running around trying to demolish every relationship Maddox had, we were destroying potential allies we could use in this war. Now, just the two of us were left...and Maddox owned us both. We had done his dirty work, and he'd just waited until we were done.

So fucking stupid.

I'd walked right into his trap...again.

Damien sat across from me with his eyes on the concrete floor. His arms were crossed over his chest, and his suit was wrinkled from his slouched posture. He hadn't said more than two words since Maddox and his crew left. He normally couldn't shut his mouth for more than ten seconds, but now he was speechless.

That wasn't a good thing.

It was my job to kill the man who'd tortured my family, and now I was in business with the motherfucker. I couldn't kill him because of the repercussions, and I couldn't walk away from him either because the consequences would be the same.

What the fuck was I going to say to Sofia?

Damien lifted his gaze and looked at me. "What the fuck are we gonna do?"

It was one of the first times I was glad we were a *we* rather than just being an *I*. Maddox was an enemy I couldn't defeat, a problem I couldn't solve. I felt inadequate. I felt like a terrible excuse for a man. "I have no goddamned idea."

"We have to play by his rules if we want to keep Sofia safe, not to mention save our own asses. But can we deal with a motherfucker like him every day? He makes it seem like we'll be business partners, but you know he's gonna be a little bitch the whole time."

I nodded in agreement.

"But I can't count the number of times we tried to kill him. It exploded in our faces every single time. Just when we think we have him by the balls, we don't. If we make that same mistake again, we won't be able to live with the consequences."

At least I didn't have to keep Damien on a leash this time. He wasn't going to gamble with my wife's safety...not again. "I agree. We'll just have to deal with it."

"Unless he would let us depart from the business altogether..."

If that were the case, Maddox would have shot me on the

spot. "No, he wants us under his thumb. If he just wanted our business, he could've taken that away a long time ago."

Damien looked at the ground again. "So, that's it? We just let it be?"

We had no other choice. "Yes."

Damien ran his hand along his jawline. "What are you gonna do about Sofia?"

"What do you mean?"

"Well, she's never going to approve of this."

It didn't matter whether she approved or not. This was the only way to keep everybody safe. It had to be this way, even though I hated it. "She'll deal with it. She has to."

26

SOFIA

I WAS SITTING AT THE TABLE WORKING ON MY COMPUTER when Hades walked inside. He was a man of few words, but his moods were so palpable, he didn't need to say much to express his feelings. He didn't look at me or greet me as he stepped inside and stripped off his jacket. It was like I didn't exist, like he wished I weren't home.

I knew his anger had nothing to do with me, but I didn't appreciate it either way.

He loosened his watch and set it on the dresser.

I was working on a spreadsheet for the hotel, but it could wait until later. I closed the laptop and leaned forward in the chair.

Hades dragged his feet as long as he could. He slipped off his shoes and yanked off his tie. His fingers slowly unbuttoned his collared shirt, and he left a pile of clothes on the closet floor. He stepped back into the bedroom, standing in just his slacks. His muscled physique was more swollen than usual, as if he'd just gone to the gym for a rigorous workout. All he had to do was be angry, and he gave himself a workout of a lifetime. He took a seat in the other armchair, his body pivoted slightly away from me. He leaned back into the chair, one arm on the table.

Then we sat in silence for a long time. I stared at my husband's visage, seeing the tightness of his jaw, the emptiness of his eyes. I knew he was troubled by the events of the day, and since nothing got him as worked up as Maddox, I knew he was the culprit behind my husband's irritation. "What happened?"

He didn't give an explanation. Instead, he rubbed his flattened palm across his jawline. I didn't like him when he was angry, but he was somehow even more attractive when he brooded like that.

I continued to wait.

"Everything happened."

"What's that supposed to mean?"

Hades didn't draw out the truth like this. He held the silence because he didn't want to admit what was going on. The longer he waited, the longer our lives would seem normal… or at least, somewhat normal. "My plans backfired. I thought I was making movements in the right direction. Instead, I got cornered."

What was that supposed to mean?

"I thought I had Maddox taken care of…"

Anytime his name was mentioned, I felt sick to my stomach. I almost asked Hades never to say that name in my presence, but that just gave Maddox power over me. It just made me weak, made me a victim.

"He cornered Damien and me at the lab. Now that all of our competitors have been disposed of, Maddox has decided to join the business. He infiltrated my men, has me outnumbered, and now I have no choice but to let him in."

I never foresaw anything like this happening. I couldn't even process what he'd just told me. War meant one side had to die, not that both sides would converge together. "I don't understand. You're in business with him?"

He nodded. "Now we run the same drug empire together."

There had to be something I was missing. "And when he drops his guard, you're going to kill him?"

Hades wouldn't look at me.

"You're going to kill him, right?" I started to panic, started to hear the emotion in my voice. I refused to live in a world where Maddox and my husband were allies. I'd kill him myself before I let that happen.

Hades held his silence.

I used words he had said to me so many times. "Look at me."

He resisted me at first, but he slowly turned to meet my

gaze. There was sadness, apology in his look. His eyes shifted back and forth like he was fighting to keep himself from looking down at the ground.

"Tell me you're going to kill him."

"Baby…" He took a deep breath, visibly wincing as the air left his lungs. "I can't."

"Yes, you fucking can." I slammed my hand down on the table. "We don't forgive and forget. We don't sweep it under the rug and pretend it never happened. You told me that we were gangsters, that we were loyal to each other. Letting him walk away is not fucking loyalty. Who are you? You are not the man I married."

Pain moved into his gaze, as if I'd hurt him all the way down to his core. "You don't understand…"

"I don't understand?" I asked incredulously. "That man raped your wife. You have no idea the shit he did to me. You have no idea how he would grab me by the neck and shove my face into the mattress and then…"

Hades jumped to his feet. "Stop." It was the first time he'd raised his voice, so it sounded like he was yelling at me. He usually commandeered a conversation simply by changing his tone. But this time, he snapped. His hand moved over his face, and he sniffed audibly, as if he were controlling his unspent tears.

I pitied him as I stared at him, but I was still enraged.

Hades was quiet for a long time as he considered what to say. He breathed hard as he battled his emotions to reach pragmatism. "I would kill him if I could. You have no idea how much I want that. But every time I made a move against him, I always lost. And if I make a move against him now... I just can't."

"Why not?"

He stared at the floor. "Because he'll take you..."

My heart started to thud in my chest. All the adrenaline and anxiety came rushing back. I never thought about my time with Maddox, but I hadn't forgotten every little detail of my captivity.

Hades continued talking. "I know he'll make good on his threat. If I try to kill him, and I fail...I couldn't live through that again. I barely lived through it the first time. You are the most important thing to me, and if that means I have to deal with him on a regular basis, then so be it. I will not risk you."

I didn't want to go through that again under any circumstances. But I didn't want that man to be part of our lives. I didn't want my husband to have to look at him every day. I didn't want that asshole in my hotel, my family's legacy. I just couldn't accept the surrender. "I understand your decision, but we can't live that way."

"We don't have a choice. He told me he would never hurt you or our son as long as our relationship stays professional. Making me a partner was always what he wanted. Now that he has it, he won't bother us again."

"That doesn't matter. I refuse to accept the lesser of two evils. He deserves to die for what he did."

"I know…"

"How can you expect me to bump into him every time I turn around? To have him in our lives indefinitely? How can you look him in the eye without wanting to strangle him? We'll never move on if we have to live like this every day. We'll never heal."

He pivoted his body toward me and placed his hands on his hips. "We have no other choice. You never have to see him again. We can arrange for that."

"How? He's going to be at the hotel."

"I know. So, you won't be."

My heart fell into my stomach. "So, you're taking away the one thing that is mine? That hotel belongs to my family, and now I can't even step foot inside of it because of him? You expect me to accept that?"

Shame was in his eyes. "I can tell him never to go to your office, but I can't prohibit him from other places in the hotel."

"That's not the point, and you know it. If I want to keep what is mine, I have to subject myself to that cruelty. That's not right."

"I know it's not…"

"Then I don't accept it."

He gripped his skull for a second, breathing through his anger. "I hate this as much as you. I hate myself for not fixing this. I feel like a pathetic excuse for a man. But this is what we have to do. We need to make the best of it. We need to keep all of us safe. It's not just about you and me anymore… We have someone else to think about now."

My blood turned ice-cold. "Did he threaten Andrew?"

He didn't answer my question because he didn't need to.

All of this was so overwhelming that I couldn't handle it. I stepped away with my arms crossed over my chest, thinking about the terrible future I would have. Even if I played by his rules, I would never feel safe. Until Maddox was dead, I would never feel free. The only way to escape him was to escape Hades. "I'm leaving you." I stared at the wall because I couldn't meet his look. I didn't want it to come to this, but I had to protect myself and our son.

Hades was quiet, like he hadn't heard what I said.

"I can't stay here and live like that. I married you because you said you could protect me. Well, you obviously can't, so I need to move on." It hurt to say these things, but I had to do what I needed to do.

Hades moved toward me, and when he looked at me, his face looked like a raging battlefield. His vein protruded from his forehead, and there was a red tint to his face. His eyes narrowed on mine, and he stared at me with an arctic coldness. "I'm going to give you one chance to take that back." His voice was low but so deadly. He was more terrifying than Maddox ever was. He threatened me without even making a single threat.

My heart started to slam against my rib cage. This man never scared me, but when he behaved this way, it felt like my skin was melting off my bones.

"I have done nothing but take care of you since the moment you became my wife. I took your place with the expectation of death. I had offers from beautiful women every night that I was out, and I rejected them all. When you weren't ready, I stayed patient. I admit that things are difficult right now, but I have done everything I possibly can to protect you. If you really feel that way, if you really think I'm worthless, then get the fuck out of my house. Leave my name and don't come back." He stepped away from me and turned around. He grabbed a t-shirt from one of his drawers and prepared to walk out.

I shouldn't have said what I did. It was cold and heartless, but I was frustrated. If there was nothing for me here, I needed to leave. "Hades."

He stopped in front of the door but didn't turn around.

I walked up behind him and stopped when we were close together. "I'm sorry…"

He slowly turned around and faced me again. His face was still livid.

"That's not what I meant. You've been a good husband to me. That's why I fell in love with you…"

His anger slowly faded away.

"But you can't expect me to live like this. I'll never feel safe. I'll never feel whole. I understand why the risks are too high to retaliate, but rolling over and just accepting it is something I just can't do. That man would've taken everything from me. I just can't do it…"

"Like I said, we have no choice."

"I still think I should leave."

His eyes narrowed.

"If he's attached to you, then he'll never go away. But I can move to Rome and run the hotel there. I could take my mother with me and never have to think about him again. If this is the only way Andrew and I can have a new life, then we should take it."

Instead of him bursting with anger, his face started to turn white like snow. He suddenly turned cold, as if his limbs were hardening from frostbite. The light left his eyes like the sun had set and would never rise again.

"If you aren't going to kill him, then I don't know what else to do."

Hades abruptly turned around and walked out the door without looking at me. Instead of closing it behind himself, he just left it open. He walked down the hallway with sagging shoulders and a crippled physique. He looked like a man broken. Even when Maddox beat him to within an inch of his life, he'd never looked this weak. But now he looked like the walking dead.

I should go after him, but I couldn't. I was too heartbroken, too frozen to do anything about it.

SOFIA AND HADES'S STORY CONCLUDES
IN...

The conclusion to the insanely popular Betrothed Series by critically acclaimed author Penelope Sky. Hades has done everything for the woman he loves. Now it's time for Sofia to do the same for him.

I never broke the curse...I just changed it.

Now I'm forced into a partnership with Maddox, and since I can't kill him, I have to tolerate him every day.

So Sofia leaves me.

I've sacrificed everything for her, but it's never enough. My love for her doesn't change despite the betrayal. The torture continues.

What am I gonna do?

I have one option. I said no the first time, but I'm not sure I can say no again...

Order Now

Damien is getting his very own story! There will even be guest appearances from Hades and Sofia AND a crossover story featuring Heath, the new Skull King. It's just as unpredictable and riveting!

When Heath, Balto's brother, demands payment from Damien's

business, things get out of hand…and a war begins. It's the first time a character from another series has become a main player in one of my books. And it's going to be quite a tale.

Hades retired from the business.

Now it's just me.

Look at me now. Bitter…angry…depressed. I resent my former friend so much, even hate the guy, but I've never been the same since he refused to forgive me.

I meet a woman. She's like all the others…beautiful, interesting, good at the fun stuff, but I don't feel anything.

One woman will love you for you, not your money or your power, but you'll lose her. And once she's gone…she's gone.

That gypsy wasn't right about me too, right?

I've got trouble on my doorstep when the new Skull King shows up. He wants a cut of my business.

Like he's getting anything. This is all I have left.

Once again I become swallowed by the underworld.

Will I survive it?

Order Now

She's gone.

But the fortune can't be true because she means nothing to me.

Nothing at all.

But the doubt starts to creep in. My thoughts only focus on one thing. The other women no longer satisfy me.

It starts to drive me crazy.

When I finally confront her, the horror shatters me.

She's marrying someone else.

Order Now

She's mine once again but she's practically a ghost.

She's just using me...not that I mind.

But her indifference is suffocating. I mean nothing to her...less than what she used to mean to me. Admissions of regret and apologies aren't enough to fix it.

I have to return to the gypsy...and hope for the best.

Order Now

Made in the USA
Middletown, DE
13 July 2023

34922720R00165